TORRID LITTLE AFFAIR

Forbidden Desires, Book Three

KENDALL RYAN

Torrid Little Affair

Copyright © 2017 Kendall Ryan

Copy Editing and Formatting by

Pam Berehulke

Cover Design by

Okay Creations

All rights reserved. No part of this book may be reproduced or transmitted in any form without written permission of the author, except by a reviewer who may quote brief passages for review purposes only.

This book is a work of fiction. Names, characters, places, and incidents are either the product of the author's imagination or are used fictitiously.

About the Book

The best way to get over someone is to get under someone else. And I have the perfect candidate all picked out.

My new assistant is tempting beyond belief with her curvy body and take-no-shit attitude. All those luscious curves, and a juicy ass I'm already in love with. God, the things that I would do to that ass . . .

But it's the haunted look in her eyes that speaks to me. Like she's taken just as much shit in her past as I have—maybe more. We both deserve a little fun.

Love can't fix everything. Mind-blowing sex and a few killer orgasms, on the other hand?

I have a feeling those might do the trick.

Chapter One

Cooper

Six months.

Six months was all it took for me to completely lose my shit. I gave it my best shot, but it turned out all the one-night stands and hangovers in the world couldn't erase the sting of heartbreak and rejection. My brother Gavin had gotten the girl, while I'd retreated alone to the one place that had always felt like home.

While my grandparents were still alive and in my life, they owned a condo in Florida in a development that was little more than a cheap apartment complex with a bunch of gray-haired retirees. But once a year when my mom dropped us off there during spring break, something about the salty ocean air and swaying palm trees felt like heaven. Like I could escape my lonely little world and all my problems while I was there.

Which was why when I fled Boston, I'd gone to the beach house I now owned on Sanibel Island. The two-bedroom cottage felt more like home than my four-thousand-square-foot luxury apartment in the city. Mostly, though, I just wasn't ready to see Gavin and Emma yet.

Wasn't ready to face seeing them as a couple and pretend to be happy for them. Fuck that.

So I'd spent my time licking my wounds and hitting the gym. Dinner was at my favorite local beach bar, where there was usually a different tourist to take home each night. It wasn't fulfilling, but it distracted me—at least somewhat—from the heartbreak that threatened to make an appearance every time I thought of my brother with Emma.

What still killed me was that I'd let her see how much she meant to me. I'd been vulnerable with her, asked her to choose me, and yet she hadn't. That was the most crushing blow.

This mistake wouldn't be solved by hate-fucking Emma out of my system. No, I was going to have to live with the festering wound of seeing her on my brother's arm. Live with the knowledge that she'd chosen him and not me. It was the one mistake that couldn't be fixed in my life—there was no easy solution, no forgetting it and moving on. And that stung like a motherfucker.

Second place was first loser. And I knew that better than anyone.

I was just about to jump in the shower after a day spent surfing when my phone rang. It was my oldest brother, Quinn. Shutting off the water, I grabbed my cell from the counter.

"Hello?"

"Wow. He picks up."

The surprise in Quinn's voice was annoying. Accurate—because I rarely answered my phone anymore—but annoying.

"What's up, man?" I tried to keep the irritation out of my voice.

"It's time you came home."

I rolled my eyes. We'd had this conversation at least a dozen times. "And why would I do that?"

"To be blunt? Because we're going to remove you from the payroll and kick you out of the company if you don't get your ass back to Boston."

That had my full attention. I could only imagine Gavin pushing for my termination. *The prick.*

"I hired someone for you," Quinn said. "It'll be just what you need to throw yourself back into work, and I think you'll find Corinne is a huge asset."

I rolled my eyes. "Fine. I'll come back."

"Glad to hear it." I could hear the smile in Quinn's voice.

"But I'm not flying commercial. Send the jet."

Quinn released a long sigh. "Christ. When did you become so demanding?"

I ignored his question. Getting fucked over would do that to a guy. From here on out, I would call the shots. Things would be done according to my terms, or not at all. "See you soon, brother."

Stripping off my wet swim shorts, I cranked the shower faucet to hot and tried to pretend that things would be fine once I got back to Boston.

They had to be, right?

Chapter Two

Corinne

"Why aren't you dating anyone yet?" Mauve asked, adjusting the oxygen tubes that rested just below her nostrils.

We'd had this conversation too many times, and it always ended the same way—with me feeling angry at her for prying, and then later guilty about getting mad at a sick old woman who meant well. It was a ridiculous cycle I hoped to one day break.

"You know I can't do that."

She scoffed at me. "The hell you can't."

I rolled my eyes and stood to help her adjust the knob on the side of her oxygen tank. Mauve was the closest thing I had to a mother, and while I loved her to pieces, when she pried into my personal life, part of me wanted to strangle her with those oxygen tubes.

Mauve pursed her lips, waiting for me to continue the same conversation we'd had a thousand times. But nothing would ever change my mind, could ever, so I flipped open her book to the dog-eared page and took a deep breath.

"Where were we? Gideon was just about to propose, right?" I would never experience the kind of romantic love I read about in these pages, and that was fine by me. It was best left for fiction, and I did love a good romance.

"Wait." Mauve motioned for me to stop. "Aren't you going to give me anything at all?"

Since I couldn't deny an old lady her only source of weekly gossip, I lowered the book to my lap. "I started a new job this week."

Mauve smiled, her blue eyes crinkling in the corners. "Thank goodness. Tell me all about it."

Ever since the state lost funding for the inner-city orphanage where I was working, I'd spent the last two months unemployed and barely scraping by. This new job had been a huge blessing. But there was no way in hell I could tell Mauve that I now worked at an escort agency, even if I was just hired to coordinate schedules and maintain the website.

"I'm a coordinator and sit behind a computer all day, nothing too exciting, but it will pay the bills nicely. And better yet, it came with excellent benefits and health insurance." That last part was critical to me, and why I'd been so picky when job-hunting.

"I'm proud of you, kiddo."

I smiled at her and the silly nickname she'd given me when I came to live under her care at the age of thirteen. Even if she was a pain in my rear end sometimes, she was one of the few people I cared about on this earth.

"Thanks, Mauve. This week was just getting acquainted and overviews. Monday, I'll start shadowing one of the women who's worked there a while, but my new boss will be back in town, so I'm sure things will get more exciting then."

I had no idea how very true that statement was about to become.

My life was simple, and simple was good. But Mauve was right—it wasn't great. And sometimes, even I had to admit there was something missing.

Chapter Three

Cooper

After spending one last weekend on the sunny Florida coast, I'd arrived back in Boston last night and spent a restful night in my old bed. Even though I really hadn't been ready to come home yet, it seemed that at least so far, it was going okay. I was surprised to discover that I'd missed the smallest things—like my espresso machine and my steam shower and my cleaning lady. My penthouse has been kept immaculate, and for that I was grateful.

Strolling into the office on Monday morning, I waved a greeting at the receptionist and found my brothers standing inside the open area as if they were waiting for my arrival.

Quinn, my oldest brother, pulled me into a hug, clapping me loudly on the back. "He lives and breathes."

I shoved him away playfully. "I'm here."

"You're fucking tanned. Look at you." Quinn grinned at me.

I rolled my eyes, my gaze finally setting on my other brother, Gavin. He was six years older than me, closer in age to me than Quinn, but we felt a million years apart. Ever since Emma, his new wife, had strolled into these offices last year—our worlds had been turned upside down.

I knew they'd be perfect together, and so like the good younger brother I was, I'd pushed them together. Gavin had been reluctant, not wanting to get into another relationship after his last girlfriend died tragically. So I'd done the only thing I could think of to spur him into action—I'd taken her out myself and pretended I was interested in the pretty little librarian.

But after a while, I wasn't pretending. Emma won me over, and I fell hard and fast. And in the end? She'd chosen the man standing before me.

"We missed you around here," Gavin said, surprising me. His embrace was quick, really just a half hug and a thump on the back, but it was a warm and unexpected surprise.

"There's a peace offering waiting for you in your office." Quinn shot me a lopsided grin.

"Thanks, man." I shook Quinn's hand again and wandered to the coffee machine where a fresh pot was already brewing. A waited a moment for it to stop, then poured myself a mugful.

It felt good to be back, better than I would have thought. The familiar scent of coffee hung in the air, and in the background, I could hear the tapping of fingers against keyboards. It was structured and orderly, and I decided that might be a good thing. My nights spent chasing a bottle of bourbon, the marathons of meaningless sex, and days spent nursing a hangover couldn't go on forever. Not that my cock minded much, but my liver? That was another story. I wasn't even thirty yet, but I often felt sluggish and tired.

Pushing those thoughts away, I rounded the corner to my office with its wall of floor-to-ceiling windows overlooking the downtown skyline. It was comforting, familiar, but the view wasn't what captured my attention.

True to his word, it appeared that Quinn had gotten me a welcome gift.

A young woman sat perched in the chair in front of my sleek glass-and-chrome desk, her hands neatly folded in her lap. Honey-blond hair fell to just below her shoulders. Her breasts were full and round, and she was dressed in a black pencil skirt and a pale pink silk blouse.

I might still be bitter about how the last several months had played out, but I wasn't too far gone not to take a bite of this apple. I was still a man, after all.

I cleared my throat, causing her head to snap in my direction.

"Hello, Mr. Kingsley."

She had wide blue eyes and a full, pouty mouth, and she was staring at me, waiting for a response.

"It's Cooper. And you are?"

A distraction.

My new little fuck-toy.

She rose to her feet, standing before me in a pair of four-inch heels that did nothing to even out our massive height difference. "I'm Corinne O'Neil. Your brothers hired me. They thought—"

"I know what they thought. They thought I needed a good, hard fuck, and they sent you in to do the job. Is that it?"

I ran my thumb along the side of her cheek as Corinne shuddered and let out a gasp. She staggered back a step, bracing her hands against the desk behind her.

"Sir?"

I cocked my head, studying her in amusement. "You are the new girl, correct? The one they hired just for me?"

"Yes, but . . ."

"But what?" I closed the distance between us, stroking her cheek again, appreciating how soft it felt, and how warm and pink it grew under my appraisal. "Instead of dropping to your knees to take my cock in your mouth, you're going to act all shy and embarrassed? Save it. There's no need for games. Not with the amount we're paying you."

Twin blotches of color appeared high in her cheeks.

"Get on with it," I barked, tugging open my belt.

Corinne burst into tears and fled from my office.

What the fuck?

After quickly latching my belt, I gave chase. But when she disappeared into the ladies' room, I stopped, breathing hard and with my fists clenched at my sides.

I waited a few moments but Corinne didn't emerge, so I stalked over toward Alyssa's desk. She was Gavin's executive assistant, and was someone who could be relied upon. Even for something delicate like this.

"Did you need something?" she asked when I stopped in front of her desk.

"Actually, yeah." I paused, rubbing the back of my neck. "I think I fucked up. The new girl, Corinne? I'm pretty sure she's in the bathroom crying because of me right now."

Alyssa frowned.

"Don't let her leave, okay? Not until I apologize."

"Okay." She rose from her chair, grabbing a box of tissues from the edge of her desk, and headed toward the restroom.

As thankful as I was that she hadn't asked what I'd done to make Corinne cry, I knew I needed to out myself to at least one person.

"Hey, what's up?" Quinn asked as I stopped in front of his desk.

I dropped into the seat in front of him, feeling like my workday had gone on a lot longer than fifteen minutes. Jesus, was that all it had been since I'd arrived in the lobby, feeling so hopeful about my future?

I was a hot fucking mess.

"So . . . about the gift you left in my office?"

He stopped typing and looked up at me. "Yes?"

I swallowed a heavy lump in my throat. "She was for?"

His heavy brows drew together. "She's meant to be your new assistant. She's more than qualified. And if she does well, my hope is that she can take over the office manager position. She's been training for this week with Alyssa, and has caught on very quickly."

"Fuck." I pinched the bridge of my nose, feeling the stirrings of a headache.

"What does that mean? Did something happen?"

Blowing out a frustrated sigh, I lifted my gaze to his. "Yeah. Sort of."

And by sort of, I mean I nearly pulled out my cock and forced it into her pretty mouth. Jesus.

"Talk, man. I've got a conference call starting in three minutes."

"When you said gift . . ." I waggled my eyebrows. "And I saw a pretty young thing sitting in my office . . ."

He wasn't catching on. I was going to have to spell it out for him.

"I thought she was there for sex—to help me blow off some steam."

"Jesus, Cooper," Quinn growled. "Tell me you didn't proposition her?"

I looked down at my newly shined shoes.

"Fuck," he roared.

"It was a mistake. But honestly, dude, you never said you'd hired me an assistant. You said you'd gotten me a gift. Think about it." I raised my eyebrows again.

But Quinn was shaking his head. "You're here to work, not to blow off steam or whatever you call it. I assume that's what you spent the last six months doing on the beach."

"Again, my mistake."

"So, what happened?"

"Well . . ."

"Don't fuck with me, Cooper. What happened exactly." He annunciated each word as though it was its own sentence.

"I propositioned her for sex, and she ran from my office crying."

"Goddamn it." Quinn rose to his feet and stalked toward the windows where he gazed down on the traffic below, his hands in his hair.

"I'm going to fix it. I just wanted you to know."

"Good. Then what are you still doing in my office?" he asked, turning to face me again.

I nodded and rose to my feet, heading to the door and wondering if Alyssa had coaxed Corinne from the bathroom yet. And if she had, exactly what I was going to say.

The deep rumble of Quinn's voice made me pause at the doorway.

"And, Cooper? You can find women to fuck on your own time."

"Understood."

He nodded. "Now, go make this right."

I would. I had to. I couldn't live with myself if Corinne quit because of my disgustingly chauvinistic behavior.

That wasn't me. It wasn't who I was. I'd always been the nice guy women could trust, the one who made them feel safe and comfortable, and even cherished. I certainly wasn't some creeper only interested in sex.

When I approached Alyssa's desk, Corinne was there—looking incredibly delectable in her fitted skirt that accentuated her curves and made my knees go weak. She had a body built for sin, and the caveman in me wanted to drag her back into my office and show her how amazing those God-given curves could be used, devoured, worshipped.

My brain might have thought that I was still nursing a heartbreak over losing Emma, but my body? My body had moved on, quickly cataloging the differences between the two women and deciding which was superior.

First, there was Emma, who was slender and delicate—*and my brother's fucking wife*, my subconscious reminded me. She was graceful, beautiful even, but she sure as hell had never gotten my blood pumping like Corinne had managed to do in the few minutes we'd spent together.

Corinne was . . . well, in a league of her own. Her body was thicker, healthy in a way that was biologically pleasing on the most basic level to me as a man. She had ripe, heavy breasts and a slim waist, but luscious hips and a juicy ass that I was already in love with.

Fuck. The things that I would do to that ass . . .

She looked as though she was meant to birth children, to nurse them, to care for them. At the most primitive level, I wanted her, wanted to fill her with come and . . .

My thoughts slammed to a halt.

Shit.

Pull yourself together, Coop.

I wasn't supposed to be fantasizing about her—I was supposed to be plotting a way to reassure her and keep her on my team. For work. Nothing more.

Jesus. I needed to get a hold of myself.

I drew a sharp inhale, noticing the way the skin on her face and neck was pink and blotchy. She was upset and had only just stopped crying, by the looks of it.

"I messed up. Can I speak with you for a moment?"

I asked, my voice soft.

Alyssa gave her an encouraging smile as if to say, *Don't worry. Despite his aggressive behavior, he's not a rapist. Promise.*

Corinne nodded and headed into my office. I followed a safe distance behind her and left the door open.

"I am sorry. So fucking sorry. That was a misunderstanding." My words came out in a rush. "My brother said he'd gotten me a gift, and I read into it. It was a massive mistake on my part."

Corinne looked me over, her expression suspicious. "Do your brothers often give you women as gifts?"

I shook my head. "No. Never. I'm just a little fucked up right now, after some past . . . relationship stuff. And when I saw you, I thought maybe they were trying to cheer me up."

She sniffed again, eyeing me warily. "I see. I'm sorry I freaked out like that."

I shook my head. "Don't apologize. You had every right to."

Corinne looked down at the chair in front of my desk, and I gestured for her to sit. When she did, I took the chair next to her, rather than the one behind my desk. I thought it might seem less threatening to sit beside her, rather than across from her, but I hadn't counted on the close proximity this would force us into.

"You're not going to quit, are you?" I asked.

Corinne shook her head. "I need this job. The pay is great and the health benefits are amazing. And so far, well, I really enjoyed it."

So far—as in, before I'd gotten into town.

"That's good. I just want to make sure you'll be comfortable working with me."

She nodded. "I'm not going to break from one pickup line. I'm actually pretty embarrassed at how I reacted."

That was interesting. It was the last thing I expected her to say. "You have nothing to be embarrassed about."

She gave me a shy smile. "Thanks." Then she let out a shaky breath, and her gaze drifted from mine. "Should we get to work, or . . ."

"First—and tell me to fuck off if I'm out of line here—but I'd like to know why when I came on to you, you looked scared. But you also looked curious."

She mumbled something I couldn't hear, and her gaze drifted to the floor.

"I saw it, Corinne, and I'm just curious. Care to tell me why?"

Her lips parted in surprise, but she didn't respond. Several tense moments ticked past.

"Tell me to fuck off, Corinne. I don't want to make you uncomfortable." *Any more uncomfortable than I already have, anyway.*

She raised one hand, holding her palm toward me. "No. It's just, I'm . . . it's a fair question."

Reading the situation as one that may call for a little more privacy, I rose and crossed the room, closing the door most of the way, but not completely. "Please enlighten me then." I returned to the seat beside her.

"You have to know the effect you have on women." She waved a hand in my direction. "You're . . ."

"I'm what?" I couldn't help the smile playing on the

edges of my lips. This felt a lot like flirting, and as out of practice as I was, she had all my attention.

She straightened her shoulders. "Attractive. And I guess I was the tiniest bit flattered by your offer. I haven't ... haven't been with a man in that way in a very long time. Haven't felt desired."

"I see." Her words made my pulse spike, and my desire to claim her raged even brighter. "Why haven't you been with a man? Because, excuse me for being so blunt, but you're fucking stunning. Surely, you don't lack for offers."

Her cheeks flushed and she looked down at her hands briefly before meeting my eyes again. "I have some hang-ups when it comes to sex. God, I can't believe I'm telling you this."

"Don't be embarrassed. I just had my heart forced through a shredder, and I admitted that to you within the first few minutes of us talking."

She picked at the polished edge of her thumbnail. "I'm not sure what it is about you—talking to you—that makes me feel like I can open up."

"You can," I assured her. It was crazy, but I knew

just what she meant. We weren't shy or timid around each other like two people who'd just met ought to be. Instead, our eye contact was direct, and our words were honest and bare. It was exhilarating.

I decided to press her. Leaning closer, I asked, "What kind of hang-ups, Corinne?"

She swallowed, her delicate throat working. "Just nerves more than anything. Not only am I out of practice, but the experiences I had early on weren't . . . healthy."

"I'm sorry."

"Don't be." She shook her head, obviously not wanting my pity. I knew that feeling.

I rose to my feet, offering her my hand to draw her up with me. "I'm sorry that you were ever treated as anything other than a goddess. And I'm very sorry that you haven't found someone special to make you feel good, to bring you pleasure, to erase those sour memories."

She nodded, her gaze locked on mine. And, Christ, if I didn't know better, I would have thought she wanted me to kiss her. Her lips parted and her tongue darted out to wet her full bottom lip.

Clearly, my ability to read a woman's signals were off. Like, way fucking off. I shoved my hands in my pockets and forced myself to take a step back.

This was insane. Totally fucking insane. But the longer that Corinne stood here, watching me with those sad eyes, and knowing that she'd been treated poorly, hearing her admit she hadn't been properly taken care of—it did something to me.

Since I'd already managed to make an ass of myself once this morning, the logical side of me knew the last thing I should do was latch onto this moment and push for more. I knew that deep in my soul. But I also knew that I was a Kingsley, a man of action, not words. I could help Corinne, and in turn, she could help me.

"Cooper?" she asked, still standing in the center of my office, watching me closely.

"What if I could help you?"

Corinne's eyes widened.

"Don't freak out. Just listen."

I placed a hand on her shoulder and guided her back to her seat. It was probably better that she was sitting down for this conversation, because I was pretty sure I'd lost my mind.

"I'm a fucking mess. Obviously." I flashed her a smile. "Despite your first impression of me, I promise I know how to make sure a woman is comfortable, how to bring her pleasure. I know how to read a woman's signals, which positions are the most enjoyable, how to make her come, when to press her for more, when to ease up. I might not have a fancy business degree, but that shit I know. Better than any man out there, I'd wager. And despite reading the situation wrong before, that's a promise."

She swallowed again, her throat bobbing and her eyes not daring to stray from mine. I had her complete attention.

"Just hear me out." I wandered from my spot near her chair toward the windows that looked out on the bustling city below. The hum of traffic, the hustle as people and cars and buses all jockeyed for position, all the chaos below seemed to illustrate my situation even more.

It was crazy, but it made a mad sort of sense for us both to explore the simple pleasures life had to offer, to take a step back from it all and just give in. It was a long shot, but something about Corinne—her brokenness that I recognized all too well, her vague interest in me—made me certain I should offer her this. I *had* to. I couldn't live with myself if I let her walk away, so sad and lonely and curious.

"This could be good for both of us," I said, turning to face her again.

"What are you proposing?" Her arched brows rose even more in wonder.

"I'll make you feel good. No strings. No messy entanglements. Just sex."

God, I sounded so cliché. If this moment had a theme song, it would be "Sexual Healing" by Marvin Gaye.

"But you're my boss," she blurted after several long seconds.

"During the workday, yes. But outside of work hours—nights, weekends—I'm just a man and you're just a woman."

Her pulse thumped steadily in her throat, but she shook her head. "I can't . . . That's . . ."

"I can see how timid you are, little dove. Just promise me you'll think it through."

Corinne's eyes strayed from mine, leaving me to wonder what in the actual fuck I'd just done.

Chapter Four

Corinne

It's safe to say that day one with Cooper Kingsley didn't go the way I'd planned. If I'd known how forward this man would be—or how nervous the sound of his low, demanding voice would make me feel—I would have never taken this job.

I avoided Cooper's eyes, staring instead at the patch of gray carpet between my feet while a million thoughts raced through my head.

I hardly even recognized myself around him. Maybe it was because it had been so long since anyone propositioned me in that way, but I hadn't felt like that around a man since . . . well, never, I guess. There was just something about his cool, steady gaze traveling up and down my body, and his large, nimble fingers unbuckling his belt that made my knees weak—and made me want to run ten thousand miles in the opposite direction.

I'd been nervous around attractive men before, their wandering gazes giving me the bad kind of butterflies. But when Cooper started unzipping his pants? I've never reacted so viscerally to a man in my life. As insane as it sounded, I felt lit up from the inside out, desired and sexy and oh-my-God turned on.

What kind of offer was that anyway? He wanted to help me overcome my fear of physical intimacy? Who did he think he was? A sex god who'd make my problems disappear with a single wave of the magical wand between his legs?

Yeah, this conversation with Cooper was doing weird things to my head.

I tucked my hair behind my ear, clearing my throat before looking up at him hesitantly. He smiled gently at me in a way that made me feel a little dizzy, so I looked back at the floor and tried to think of something to say.

"Listen, I'm sure you mean well, but I don't think it's a good idea to get involved with anyone from work, let alone my boss," I said, struggling to meet his sympathetic gaze.

Cooper took a step toward me, so I took a step back.

He raised his hands in surrender, scrunching his eyebrows together with genuine concern.

"I'm not asking for a relationship, Corinne. I'm not asking for anything, really. I just think we might be able to help each other out. In a strictly physical way," he added with a slight shrug, his tone bold and clear.

I nodded, rubbing my hands over my forearms. I couldn't help but wonder what was in it for him. Sex without strings seemed like a pretty good deal for most men, really, but I was suspicious. Why did Cooper Kingsley, of all people, with his tall, imposing frame and sexy, wounded eyes, need to ask his sex-scared employee for a few awkward nights in his bed?

But what threw me off even more was the timing of his offer. Wasn't Mauve just saying I needed to put myself out there? To loosen up and get laid already?

I looked back up at Cooper and frowned. He was sexy, there was no denying it. I hadn't been this attracted to someone in years. But I couldn't silence the little voice in the back of my head screaming that I needed to get out of there. And fast.

"I really don't think it's a good idea," I said again,

wrapping my arms around myself.

Cooper nodded and leaned back to sit on the edge of his desk. "I understand," he said, running his hand over the dark wood.

I turned to leave but before I reached the door, his voice made me turn back around again.

"Just promise me one thing, Corinne. Take some time to think it over. If you gave me a chance to show you what a real physical connection could be like . . . I really don't think you'd regret it."

I paused for a moment, biting the inside of my cheek. Finally, I nodded and quickly turned to leave, grateful that the rest of the day would be mostly training and wouldn't involve any more conversations with my boss. Because, holy shit, I needed out of this man's office, out of his intense gaze, away from his maddeningly delicious cologne.

Six feet, four inches of cocky asshole, that's what he was. God, why hadn't I told him to shove his offer up his ass, and then stormed out?

Because you were intrigued.

I wanted to stab that little voice in my head right in

the throat.

It didn't matter that he was hot. That was immaterial. This was the most ridiculous proposal.

Hating myself for admitting I thought he was attractive, and hating myself even more that I'd admitted my unsavory sexual past, I pushed our entire conversation from my brain and sidled up to Alyssa, ready to get back to work.

"You okay now?" she asked.

"Perfectly fine. We were covering the annual budget, remember?" I prompted her.

"Right."

If only I could get my brain to focus on the spreadsheet in front of me instead of the gorgeous man on the other side of the wall.

• • •

I kept busy, focusing intently on everything Alyssa told me, and before I knew it, the day was over. I left the office without saying good-bye to Cooper, unsure how to act around him after what we'd last talked about.

Before heading home, I stopped at the grocery on

the way to pick up the ingredients for tonight's dinner. Once home, I wrangled all the groceries into my arms, making sure to leave at least one hand free to turn the doorknob.

"Aaron?" I called out as I opened the door, toeing off my shoes and trudging inside with the grocery bags.

He was the quietest, neatest roommate you could ever imagine, and mostly kept to himself. Wheelchair bound, Aaron watched TV or sat by the window while I was at work, petting his therapy dog, Ollie.

A freak accident several years ago had paralyzed him from the waist down, and a massive head injury reduced his mental abilities to that of about an eight-year-old. He was nonverbal and needed help in his daily care, but a nurse came for him every day while I worked, so he really was no trouble at all. In fact, if he weren't here, I'd miss the whir of his breathing treatment machine, or the soft way he hummed when he took his bath.

Plus, there was something about sharing the apartment with him and Ollie that made me feel safer. Maybe it was that we'd shared the same routines for years. Growing up the way I did, I craved the familiar, liked a routine. I certainly didn't want to go changing things around just because our arrangement was unorthodox.

Ollie greeted me first, and after I set the bags on the counter, I found Aaron sitting on the balcony, watching the birds peck at the bird feeder hanging nearby. His nurse was folding laundry in a basket beside him, and she smiled at me too.

"Thanks, Tabitha," I said.

"He's no problem at all, but you know that."

I nodded, watching as she headed back inside with the basket balanced on her hip.

"Hey." I placed my hand on his shoulder and gave it a squeeze. His eyes met mine, and he gave me a tilted smile. "We're having your favorite for dinner."

After another squeeze to his shoulder, I headed back inside to begin cooking. Tabitha called out her good-bye, and I heard the front door close. As my fingers mashed and mixed raw ground beef, my brain wandered back to today's encounter at the office.

I couldn't put my finger on it, but something about Cooper's offer made me feel naked and exposed. It wasn't just that he was suggesting carefree, emotionless sex, though that fact did nothing to make me feel better about things. No, it was the way he responded when I told him about my past. He'd instantly softened and looked so disgusted with himself, I almost wanted to comfort him.

Almost.

I still couldn't tell if it was all an act—maybe he played this scene out with every new employee his brothers threw his way. Come on way too strong, offer a shoulder to cry on when she freaks out, then coax her into giving him exactly what he wanted.

But that was where things got even more confusing. He could be a sex-addicted sociopath, which would explain how he was so good at making this arrangement sound so appealing. Then again, that didn't seem like him either—I hardly knew him at all—and yet something about him seemed so real and genuine and honest.

I sighed and set the raw meat to the side, grabbing a handful to form into a patty. The only thing I knew for certain was that I had some thinking to do. And a lot of it.

• • •

Friday morning at work, I walked straight to Cooper's office, intent on setting a few matters straight. I wasn't ready to make a decision yet, but I sure as hell needed to make sure I knew exactly what was at stake.

But no matter how determined I was to be confident and assertive in front of Cooper, I couldn't stop my hands from shaking as I opened the door to his office. I hated confrontation of any kind, especially when it happened with tall, attractive men who wanted something from me. Especially because he wanted that poor neglected spot between my legs.

I opened the door to find Cooper sitting at his desk, lost in thought as he stared at his computer screen. For a moment, I let myself take him in, admiring the hard planes of muscles under his crisp, dark blue button-down. I cocked my head to the side, noticing for the first time how green his eyes were. They were cool and focused in that moment, probably analyzing the company's financials or the latest escort schedule, but I could just make out the faintest crinkles at their corners, the telltale of someone who smiled a lot.

Suddenly, those green eyes snapped up at me, equal parts bewildered and amused at the look on my face, which I could only imagine was dumb and intrusive.

"Corinne," Cooper said with a grin. "What can I do for you?"

I immediately stood up straight and entered his office, closing the door behind me. He motioned to the chair in front of his desk but I shook my head, smoothing my black pencil skirt over my thighs.

"This won't take long," I said, ignoring the knot quickly forming in my stomach.

"Have you made your decision?" he asked, his voice calm.

"Actually, no. I haven't made a decision yet. I'm here to clarify the stakes." I surprised even myself with how sure and confident I sounded.

Cooper sat up straighter and almost seemed to be suppressing a smile. I couldn't tell if he was intrigued or entertained by me, so I chose to believe the latter, just to be safe.

Not waiting for him to answer, I continued. "I need this job. And I need to know whether my employment status hinges on me agreeing to have sex with you."

At that, any trace of a smile vanished from Cooper's face, and he looked at me with a grim, serious expression.

"I would never do that," he said, almost to himself. He cleared his throat, obviously shaken by what I'd said. "Corinne, I would never fire you for choosing not to have sex with me. I apologize—sincerely—if I gave you the impression that I'd throw you out on the street if you declined my offer."

Relieved, I let out a breath and relaxed my shoulders a bit. I nodded and did my best to keep it together.

"Okay," I said, dropping my gaze to the floor. "Thanks. I, uh, still need more time, though, before I make my decision." I fidgeted with the hem of my cardigan, fully aware of how awkwardly my words were coming out.

"Of course," Cooper said, folding his hands in his lap. "Take all the time you need, little dove. My offer still stands." His tone had softened and so had my insides—liquefying into jelly as I stood there.

I nodded and stood there timidly for a moment, unsure of what else to say. It quickly felt like I was lingering too long, so I blurted a hasty "I should probably get to work" before bolting out of his office again.

I marched straight to the bathroom, needing some

time and space to myself. I washed my hands in the sink, reveling in the coolness of the water on my warm and sweaty palms.

Looking up, I frowned at my reflection in the mirror. My face was beet red from the stress and embarrassment of confronting Cooper, and I was mortified by how visible my true feelings were.

After drying my hands, I smoothed my hair and pressed my cooled-down hands to my face. When my cheeks had calmed down to their normal rosy pink, I sighed and pushed back my shoulders, taking a deep breath in. Once I felt settled, I left the bathroom, prepared for another day of training.

It was silly, but knowing that Cooper wasn't that kind of man—the kind who would hold my job over my head for sex—made me feel way less anxious about this decision. I still had no idea whether this arrangement was something I was okay with, let alone something I wanted, but now I was sure about one thing.

Whether I chose to be with him or not, Cooper Kingsley would leave one heck of an impression on me.

Chapter Five

Cooper

Holy shit.

Once Corinne left my office, I let out a long sigh, running my hands roughly over my face. It was clear from the conversation we'd just had that there was still a lot for me to learn about this girl, whether she agreed to my offer or not.

My cock twitched at the thought of Corinne saying yes, of her melting in my arms and allowing me to have my way with her. At first, I thought she was simply a timid little bird seeking shelter, but now I wasn't so sure.

The way she came marching in here, armed with the confidence to make sure I met her demands? It was sexy as hell, and exactly the side of her I needed to see to know that she could handle what I wanted to give her.

Oh, the things I want to give her.

Before I could get carried away in my thoughts, I quickly stood up, stretching out my neck and shoulders. If I was serious about keeping my sex life and work life separate—even if they both involved the same gorgeous, fascinating woman—I needed to focus while I was at work, not fantasize about all the ways I planned to introduce Corinne to a healthy and satisfying sex life.

As I walked to Quinn's office to go over Corinne's file, which I'd wanted to review and hadn't gotten the chance to yet, I struggled to suppress a tiny lingering thought in the back of my mind. Maybe someone like Corinne with her wide, concerned eyes and soft, gentle manner was exactly what I needed to get out of this funk I'd been in since Emma.

Before I could explore that thought further, I arrived at Quinn's office, offering a single knock before opening the door.

"Hey, man, what's up? You work out your misunderstanding with Corinne?" Quinn asked, raising an eyebrow and shooting me a lopsided grin. He leaned back in his chair and crossed his arms, obviously pretty damn pleased with himself.

"Yeah, we're all good," I said, ignoring his mischievous smirk. I didn't plan on keeping my newest proposition to Corinne a secret, but now didn't feel like the right time to get Quinn up to speed on my plan. "Still, I was thinking I'd like to take a look at her file, just to be sure she's the right fit."

Quinn eyed me for a moment, trying to size up my emotions, but quickly gave up and pulled Corinne's file out of the stack of papers in front of him. "I figured you'd need confirmation," he said, tossing the file in front of me.

I opened the manila folder and scanned the first few pages, which contained her standard cover letter and résumé. Flipping further into the stack, I frowned at its contents. As I'd expected, Quinn had done a full background check on her, just like we did with all new employees. And Corinne's past was even worse than I thought.

She grew up in an orphanage outside the city, and started working the second anyone would hire her. Her file didn't suggest she'd had to resort to anything illegal or unsavory, but it was clear that her life had never been glamorous or easy.

What I read in her file, along with the history of abuse she'd hinted at, made it clear just how broken this woman really was. The realization made me feel even worse about how forceful and aggressive my initial come-on was toward her. Sure, we had plenty of girls come through here with rough and troubled pasts, but something made Corinne different. I thought I felt it when she burst into my office that morning, and after reading her file, it was clear to me what it was—Corinne and I were both lost and broken souls in need of someone to help us find our way.

"So, what do you think?" Quinn asked, his low voice interrupting my thoughts.

I cleared my throat and rolled my shoulders, pushing aside the deep thoughts still swimming through my head. "She'll do just fine," I muttered as I snapped her file closed and placed it back on Quinn's desk.

I pressed my lips together in a hard, thin line, determined not to let my feelings show. If I gave Quinn an inch, he'd take a mile—and would demand to know what my plans with her entailed exactly. Since I was still figuring that out myself, I wasn't ready to discuss it.

Quinn studied me for a moment, squinting as he leaned back in his chair. "Something's different with you," he said, pursing his lips. I didn't respond, instead shooting him a somewhat annoyed look. "I mean, besides the whole fleeing-the-city-due-to-a-broken-heart thing. Why don't you come over for dinner tonight after work?" he offered, his tone equal parts friendly and serious. "I think you and I have some catching up to do."

After some continued light teasing, I agreed to join Quinn for dinner, if for no other reason than to appease his nosiness. I still hadn't decided whether to tell him about the proposal I'd made to Corinne. Part of me longed for the guidance of a wise older brother, while another part of me knew that Quinn was just as clueless about love and acceptance as I was.

But it was clear that he already knew something was up, so maybe dinner was as good a time as any to get him up to speed. After he'd had a couple of cocktails, preferably.

The day passed by quickly, and as I finished up the last of my work and made my way to the parking lot, my stomach grumbled as I climbed into my car. If nothing else, I was looking forward to Quinn's cooking.

• • •

When I arrived at Quinn's place, he greeted me with a smile and a brisk clap on the back.

"Steak night," he said, leading me to the kitchen.

"The meat's resting, and the mushrooms are almost done. Help yourself to a drink."

I let myself into Quinn's liquor cabinet, my gaze roaming lazily over the bottles. Quinn had made sure to stock up on my favorite whiskey, so I happily poured myself a measure.

Once the food was ready, we sat down at his table to eat, our conversation light and easy. I'd been suspicious when Quinn invited me over, worried he might be staging some sort of intervention. But with how things were going so far, it was clear he really did just want to catch up.

"So," he said after a long sip of his drink, "Corinne. What do you think about her, really? Off the record. Those hips hitting you anywhere in particular?"

Yeah, those hips shot me straight in the dick, but I bristled slightly at my brother's quip. Not because I thought he said it with any malice, but because of how well he seemed to know my taste.

"She's great," I said, forcing myself to sound as normal as possible.

Quinn gave me a mischievous smile. "Come on,

Coop. I know there's more to it than that."

I sighed and swirled the liquid in my glass. This was whiskey number two, and while I didn't feel the slightest buzz yet, I knew we were at a tipping point in the night's conversation.

Fuck it.

"You're right," I said, tapping my fingers on the side of my glass. "She's special. So special, in fact, that I've offered her an exclusive no-strings-attached sexual relationship. No feelings, no commitments, just sex."

I winced once I had it all out there. Yeah, that was a lot to unload on somebody.

Quinn leaned forward, placing his elbows on the table and raising a critical eyebrow. "You did what?"

"You heard me. I made her an offer. Purely physical. She's still thinking it over."

Quinn stared at me for a moment longer before bursting into laughter. "That's about the dumbest thing I've ever heard," he said between breaths. "Out of all the women in this city you could be banging out your sadness with, you choose the one you'll have to see every day at work. You're a mess, man."

I shook my head. "No, it won't be like that. Strictly separate. At work, we'll work. Anytime outside work, we'll fuck," I said matter-of-factly, surprised by my brother's disapproval. Quinn wasn't the relationship type. Why was he, of all people, giving me shit for this?

"You'll get to know each other too well, dude. She's either gonna hate you or fall for you. Either way, you're fucked. And not in the good way," he added.

I thought again of what I read in her file, about the orphanage she grew up in.

"I'm not so worried about either of those things," I said, taking on a serious tone. "She mentioned something about demons in her past . . . I don't know the story, but it's left her with some hang-ups. She's a broken person, Quinn, and terrified of sex. To think of someone so beautiful, with so much to offer, afraid of the pleasure she could so easily receive . . . it tears at me. If this arrangement would help her, then why shouldn't I go for it? I saw the way she looked at me just before she ran— she wanted me too, it was written all over her face. She's curious, and that's what terrifies her. I'm more than happy to be the one to help her move past that fear."

I paused then, suddenly aware of the wistful look I was probably wearing. I snapped out of it and cleared my throat before draining my glass.

Quinn shrugged. "If that's how you feel, I won't stop you," he said, rising from his chair. "But I think this calls for another drink."

I followed Quinn to his library, where he poured us both a glass of brandy. We clinked glasses and each took a swig, and I relished the slight burn as the liquid slid down my throat. I examined some of the books on a nearby shelf while Quinn watched me, a concerned look on his face.

"You haven't been back in here since that night with Emma, have you?" he said.

A thin, cheerless smile spread across my face as I remembered the night when the woman I thought I loved crushed my dreams, choosing the white-hot passion of my brother Gavin over the stable love I had to offer her. Thinking of that night didn't sting as much as it used to, but it wasn't a memory I cared to linger on more than was necessary.

"No," I said, turning to face him, making as neutral a

face as possible. "How are Gavin and Emma doing?"

"Well, I think. All settled into the new place. Looks like happily-ever-after is possible for the Kingsley brothers after all."

I nodded, forcing a grim smile to my lips. After a moment, I raised my glass in the air. "To Gavin and Emma."

"To Gavin and Emma," Quinn repeated. After we both took a sip of our brandy, he swirled the liquid left in his glass before looking up at me. "Do you know what you're doing with this new girl, Coop? It sounds like you're entering into some pretty dangerous territory."

I sighed and sat in one of the plush armchairs by the fireplace. "Not a fucking clue," I muttered, running a hand over my face. "But I need this. I need to be focused on someone else for a while, I think."

Quinn nodded, then sat in the chair next to mine. "Just do me one favor, okay?" When I answered with a shrug, he said, "Talk to Gavin about this before you do anything big."

"Why would I do that?"

"You and I both know he was into the

Dominant/submissive scene before Emma. He might know a thing or two about helping a reluctant woman surrender to pleasure."

I nodded, downing the last of my brandy. Quinn had a point. Gavin would be the person to talk to about how to set up a sexual relationship based solely on one person's pleasure, especially when it came to thinking outside the box.

I left Quinn's that night with a slight buzz, both from the alcohol and the thought of embarking on a purely physical relationship with Corinne. Quinn might not have fully approved but he didn't shut me down, and I was more eager than ever to show Corinne how to unlock the pleasure within her, should she agree to my proposal. Things were looking up, and I could feel myself slowly shedding the bitterness and rage I'd been cultivating since Emma turned me down.

The only thing keeping me from feeling more excitement than I had in months?

The thought of asking Gavin, my brother and Emma's husband, for sex advice.

Fucking kill me now.

Chapter Six

Corinne

"I'm so sorry. I know I've been shadowing you for a week, but could you show me again how you did that?" I asked, leaning over Alyssa's shoulder to watch her computer screen more closely.

I had to be so annoying. Any second now, I was sure she would let out a heavy sigh or roll her eyes, but she surprised me, smiling patiently for the fiftieth time and clicking the UNDO button.

"Corinne, you seriously need to stop apologizing." Alyssa turned to give me a sympathetic grin. "I remember what my first week was like. There's a lot to take in, especially with this scheduling software. Just be patient with yourself. The Kingsley brothers run their business unlike anyone else I've ever worked for."

You got that right.

It was Monday, and I hadn't said more than "good morning" to Cooper since he told me to take my time making my decision. He had been true to his word, giving me the time and space I needed to think the whole situation through. I appreciated that fact, and I had taken my sweet time deliberating over all the pros and cons of the situation. I knew I wouldn't be able to feel secure in my decision unless I thoroughly weighed my options.

"Hey, by the way, clear your schedule for tonight," Alyssa said, flashing me a playful grin. "We're taking you to happy hour after work to celebrate the end of your first full week at Forbidden Desires."

I smiled, chuckling at the idea that I, of all people, would have a busy social calendar I'd need to clear. "Who's we?" I asked. I was ready to tell Cooper about the decision I'd reached, but I also needed to mentally prepare myself if he would be at happy hour too.

"The whole office," Alyssa said. "It's tradition. Like I said, the first week here is always crazy. I'm sure you could use a drink—or five."

I snorted and quickly threw my hand over my mouth. I wasn't exactly a lightweight, but it had been so long since I had more than one drink in a night, I could only imagine what five drinks would do to me.

But then again, I *was* looking to expand my horizons.

"What the heck," I said. "Sure, I'm in."

Alyssa smiled widely at me, and I smiled back. I was so grateful for how welcome she and all the other women who worked here made me feel.

"Perfect. Now that that's settled, let's get back to making you comfortable with our online scheduler."

By the time I finished shadowing Alyssa later that day, I had half an hour before leaving for happy hour. I sat at my desk, grateful for some time to myself before going out to socialize again. I organized the desktop on my computer, and soon my thoughts wandered back to my mental pros-and-cons list about my possible arrangement with Cooper.

Pros: I might actually have good sex. I'll have the opportunity to go as slow as I want. Cooper seems confident that he knows what to do. Did I mention good sex?

Cons: Cooper is my boss. If things go south, it'll be hard to get away from him. And if things go well, there's no way I could ever have a future with him. Once again, boss—with a capital B.

I sighed, my mind whirling from one item on the list to the next. I'd been thinking about this decision all weekend, and I was quickly becoming exhausted from trying to piece together the best course of action.

Glancing at the clock on my computer, I realized it was almost time to leave. I grabbed my purse and walked to the bathroom to freshen up before heading out for drinks.

Standing in front of the mirror, I reapplied my light pink lipstick and ran my fingers through the hair around my face. I stared at myself for a moment, taking in my rounded features. Men had told me I was pretty before, but it always felt like they were only saying it to get something out of it for themselves. Cooper made me feel that way when I first met him, but that had quickly faded when he realized how uncomfortable I was.

Our first interaction alone showed me that Cooper was more complicated than I realized. For as gruff and forward as he'd been when we first met, it was clear that there was a soft side underneath all that armor.

And it was that soft side that helped me make my final decision.

I took a deep breath and straightened the hem of my blouse. This job would be a new beginning for me in more ways than one. The thought of being in a relationship centered around my own pleasure made my stomach churn, but I knew that it was time for me to do more things that initially made me uncomfortable. The all-consuming pleasure I'd get in return was too enticing to pass up any longer. Cooper was sexy as hell, and I was more than ready to start having a normal, healthy sex life.

I was ready to say yes to Cooper's offer.

And I was ready to experience the mind-boggling pleasure I'd been denying myself for years.

Still, I knew in the back of my mind that this relationship could never go any further than sex. For as much as the physical side of things made me nervous, my life was way too complicated to even consider venturing into the emotional. The arrangement I wanted with Cooper would have nothing to do with love or affection or emotional needs. All I wanted from him was an introduction to pleasure, a chance to feel *good* for the first time in a very long time.

A knock on the the bathroom door snapped me out of my thoughts.

"Hey, Corinne, are you in there? It's time to go," Alyssa called out.

"Coming," I said, taking one last look at myself in the mirror. I looked good. And it was about time I started acting like it.

The second I stepped out of the bathroom, Alyssa turned to excitedly lead me to the parking lot. We climbed into the back of a company car, and I braced myself for my upcoming encounter with Cooper. To my surprise, Alyssa closed the door behind her and told the driver we were ready to go.

"The guys will join us in a bit," she said, rifling through her purse. "Apparently, they had some last-minute business to attend to."

I nodded and looked out the window, unsure of what to say.

Alyssa smiled. "That's typical for the Kingsley brothers, though. Always working. They're private too. I understand that what we do requires a certain level of discretion, but these guys take secrets to a whole new level," she said, checking her reflection in a small compact mirror. "It's like, what do these guys *really* have to hide, you know?"

I do *know*, I thought, but I simply chuckled and shook my head.

I might have been ready to tell Cooper about my

decision, but I didn't think it was something he'd want the whole office to know. Besides, for as kind and welcoming as Alyssa had been so far, we were nowhere near gal pals, and I didn't like the idea of a work acquaintance knowing anything about my sex life.

• • •

When we arrived at the bar, Alyssa and I sat on neighboring bar stools, and she began chatting up the bartender. She wasn't kidding when she said this was tradition—the bartender knew exactly who she was and happily gave each of us a shot of tequila on the house. Alyssa and I each took a shot glass in our hands, and she raised hers into the air.

"To surviving your first week," she said, smiling broadly at me.

"To my first week," I said back, and we clinked our glasses together before we each downed our shots. I tried not to cough as the liquid burned down my throat, then quickly bit into one of the lime wedges the bartender had provided for us.

Alyssa screwed up her face and let out a low hiss. I was glad I wasn't the only one who had a hard time with shots.

"All right, what do you ladies want to drink now?" the bartender asked, leaning forward onto his elbows and giving us a mischievous grin.

It was then that I noticed his killer biceps and the way his dark brown stubble perfectly accentuated his jawline. My decision to accept Cooper's offer had me feeling bold, so I placed my own elbows on the bar and leaned in toward the bartender, aware of how the position gave him a perfect view of my ample cleavage.

"Remind me again what the happy-hour specials are," I said in as sultry a voice as I could muster.

"What?" the bartender said loudly. "Sorry, I couldn't hear you over the music."

I giggled and leaned even closer. "I wanted to know what the specials are," I said, still trying to sound sexy, though a little more forcefully.

The bartender shook his head and placed his hand behind his ear.

"The specials!" I yelled in a voice so shrill, the bartender winced and took a step back. I could sense

Alyssa's amusement to my right, and a hot pink blush spread across my chest and up into my cheeks.

"Oh, uh, it's half-off margaritas," the bartender said. From the way he winked at Alyssa, I could tell my attempt at giving off a sensual energy had failed. Miserably.

"We'll have two margaritas," Alyssa said coolly. The bartender smiled and walked away to make our drinks.

She turned to give me a playful grin. "Corinne, I had no idea you had that in you."

I let out a low groan and hid my face in my hands. I was more than embarrassed—I was mortified. Not only because that had just happened, but because Alyssa was there to witness it. I could feel the shame spreading to my limbs, and all I wanted was for our drinks to be ready so I could numb that feeling, even just a little bit.

"Oh, come on, it wasn't that bad," she said, giving me a brisk pat on the shoulder. When I groaned again and shook my head, she said, "There are plenty of other guys in this bar. Listen, once he comes back with our drinks, we'll start looking for your next target."

Just as she stopped talking, the bartender returned with our margaritas, and Alyssa slipped him a shiny black credit card. "Leave the tab open," she said to him before turning to give me a wink. "These are on the company."

I took a long sip of my drink, relishing the cool, sour sweetness of the liquid. I could tell already that this drink would be dangerous. Even though I watched the bartender pour a good amount of tequila into the glass, all I could taste was the perfect blend of lime juice and syrup.

Alyssa turned around on her stool to survey the tables behind us, and I turned to join her, still feeling a bit wounded after my failed seduction attempt. I took a few more sips of my drink to numb the embarrassment as I let my gaze roam lazily from face to face in the bar. Apparently, this place was every business's favorite happy hour, because almost every man I saw was dressed in a crisp, well-tailored suit. Many of them looked equal parts handsome and terrifying, the kind of men who walked into a room and demanded the respect and attention of everyone in it. Alyssa started giving me some tips on how to let a guy know I was interested, pointing out particularly attractive men and explaining the strategy she would use.

It didn't take long until my head was spinning from both the tequila and Alyssa's advice. Suddenly I was grateful for the arrangement I had with Cooper. If I had to seduce a man on my own, I didn't think I'd ever be getting off ever again. Unless you counted using my own fingers.

Just as the thought of Cooper crossed my mind, he showed up at the bar like we were in a movie or something. He walked through the door, followed by his two brothers.

The three of them together was quite a sight. They were all tall and toned, but each had a special aura that differentiated him from the others. Gavin was dark and broody, while Quinn was somehow aloof and fatherly at the same time.

And then there was Cooper. I couldn't quite figure him out yet. At times, he seemed just as broody and aloof as his brothers, but there was something in his soft green eyes that made me think he might be sweeter than he first appeared. Not to mention he had the kind of body that made me weak in the knees.

I quickly realized that I was staring, and I looked away before Cooper or his brothers could catch me. Downing the rest of my drink, I did my best to make it seem like I was listening to Alyssa, but all I could think about was meeting those green eyes across the room.

Shyly, I looked back over to where the Kingsley brothers were standing. My stomach dropped as Cooper's eyes met mine with a smoldering gaze. It took everything in me to not drop my jaw then and there. We stared at each other for a moment before he broke out in a smile and started walking toward me.

"Look who decided to show up," Alyssa said loudly, waving the brothers over.

I nodded silently, unable to tear my gaze from the man I'd decided would soon be my lover.

Once Cooper was only a few feet away, I decided I needed to tell him my decision right then and there. Just as I stepped off the stool, I lost my footing, and it felt like the whole room tilted sideways. But before I could fall flat on my face, Cooper reached out and caught me, and suddenly, I was wrapped up in his arms.

A scorching blush spread over my cheeks as I looked up into Cooper's eyes and smiled shyly. "Thanks," I said, leaning into his chest for a moment as the room leveled out around me.

"No problem," he said with a smile.

We stood there for a moment before I became aware of our coworkers around us, and I quickly straightened myself and stepped out of Cooper's embrace.

"Guess I'm a little tipsier than I thought," I muttered, looking down at my shoes.

"Glad you're having fun," Quinn said politely.

I knew he was being nice, but I was so embarrassed, I couldn't even meet his gaze to thank him.

Alyssa started up a conversation with the brothers and they began an easy back-and-forth, discussing work, sports, and other things I didn't have much to say about. The longer we all stood there chatting, the more self-conscious I became, not because anyone was making me feel unwelcome, but because I was uncomfortable with how obvious it was that I was tipsy. I shifted my weight from one foot to the other, calculating how much it would cost to hail a cab to drive me home.

Cooper placed a hand on the small of my back, leaning down to speak into my ear. "Are you all right?"

I didn't respond, instead looking up into his eyes with a worried look on my face. I didn't know how to tell him that I was grateful to be there, but embarrassed and about ready to make my escape.

He gave me a soft, sympathetic smile before leaning down to my ear again. "Do you want to go home? I can give you a ride."

I nodded, and within moments, Cooper explained to everyone else that we were ready to call it a night, and he was going to drive me home. Alyssa gave me a quick hug, Gavin and Quinn both nodded and tipped their glasses, and Cooper guided me to the door with his hand on the small of my back.

Once in his car, I could feel my heart racing. If there was ever a good time to let him know I was ready for sex, it was now. He was taking me to my place, and my mind was racing with thoughts of how to get him into my bed. I could invite him in for a drink, or give him the bedroom eyes Alyssa had shown me how to do. My head was swimming with ideas, and I was grateful that Cooper, ever a man of his word, drove in perfect silence, waiting for me to say the first word.

I cleared my throat, and Cooper let his eyes wander from the road for just a moment to let me know he was listening. My heart pounding in my chest, I opened my mouth to speak.

"I, uh ... I've made my decision," I said, my voice shaking. Cooper nodded, waiting for me to continue. "My answer is yes. I think we should do this."

As the words left my mouth, we arrived in front of my place, and Cooper placed the car in park. Without saying anything, he got out and walked around the front of the car to open my door for me. When he helped me out of the car, I squeezed his hand in mine, grateful for his steadying presence.

We stood there on the sidewalk in front of my apartment, my hand in his, our faces less than a foot apart. The tension between us was palpable, and just as I was about to turn to walk to the door, Cooper pulled me into him, placing one hand behind my head, and pressed his lips softly against mine.

I tensed up for the briefest of moments, taken aback by the sudden romantic gesture. But after only a few seconds of his mouth on mine, I kissed him back, allowing my lips to part ever so slightly as his tongue touched mine. I raised one of my hands to his chest, not to push him away, but to feel his muscles underneath his shirt.

With his free hand, Cooper pulled my hips into him, and I could feel his thigh settling between my legs. The pace of our kiss quickened, our tongues moving frantically around each other, and my body responded with an instinct I didn't know it had.

Suddenly, my other hand was running through his hair, and I began grinding on his thigh. I could feel his erection pressing into my stomach, and a low moan escaped from my mouth. His hands moved over my body, brushing over my breasts and around my hips before beginning the motion again. His lips wandered to my neck, making me gasp with pleasure.

The cover of darkness made me bold. I whispered in his ear, "I want more," running my hand over the bulge in his pants.

Cooper groaned and brought his mouth back to mine, giving my bottom a gentle squeeze. "You have no idea how sexy you are," he said between kisses before placing both hands on my shoulders and pulling away to look into my eyes. "But we can't sleep together now. Not after you've had so much to drink."

I frowned and quickly closed the space between us,

crushing my mouth against his. Cooper kissed me back for a few minutes before pulling back again.

"I mean it, Corinne. There are so many things I want to do to you, trust me," he said, eyeing my body up and down. "But it wouldn't be right to do them now. If this is still what you want tomorrow, let me know. We'll work out the details."

And just like that? Cooper placed a firm yet tender kiss on my forehead and climbed back into his car, watching me unlock my front door before he pulled away.

I stumbled through my front door, my heart still racing from the intensity of that kiss. As I stood in the dark hallway, buzzing after what had just happened, there was only one thought running through my mind.

I had *definitely* made the right decision.

Chapter Seven

Cooper

"Thanks for meeting with me," I said to my brother, grateful that Emma was at work in her little bookshop and we had some privacy.

Gavin stood on the other side of his kitchen island, pouring each of us a glass of sparkling water. A smug grin spread across his face as he slid a glass of water my way. "It's not often my little brother asks me for advice these days."

I caught the glass and resisted the urge to smack that stupid look off his face, reminding myself that I needed his help, no matter how much I hated coming to him like this. Being married to Emma had softened him some, but Gavin was still an arrogant prick when I wasn't asking for advice. So, on the rare occasion that I did, he was bound to be even worse than usual.

Focus, Cooper. This is important. This is for Corinne.

I raised my glass. "Cheers, brother," I said, and Gavin nodded, clinking his glass to mine. We drank, and I was surprised by how light and refreshing the mineral water was sliding down my throat. He might be a prick, but my brother had damned good taste.

"So, what's going on, Coop? Had to be important if you, of all people, were willing to ask for help."

I shot him a dirty look and then explained my arrangement with Corinne, starting with the day I sent her running out of my office and ending with last night after happy hour, when she all but begged me to fuck her right there on the sidewalk. Gavin didn't laugh like Quinn did as I explained the situation, but I wasn't a huge fan of the way he raised his eyebrows when I told him about Corinne's troubled past.

Once I felt I'd provided adequate background information, I paused to take a sip of my water. Gavin remained silent, clearly waiting for me to actually ask him a question before speaking.

I sighed. "I was wondering if you had any advice for me as I proceed. Quinn suggested you might from your days in the Dominant/submissive scene. It's not that she doesn't get aroused—it was clear from our first meeting that her body wanted to be physical with mine. The problem is her emotional reaction to her own arousal. It scares her. And I'm just wondering if you have any tips on how to make her more comfortable with her body's natural reaction to physical pleasure."

Gavin nodded and remained silent for a moment, clearly considering what to say. When he finally opened his mouth to speak, his eyes were stern and serious.

"Before I disclose what I know about opening women up to pleasure," he said, "I want to warn you. Be careful with this one, Coop. I read her file when we hired her, and I know Quinn made sure you saw it too. She was in the system, and you and I have enough experience with that to know that you don't grow up like that without developing a few wounds over the years. She might have agreed to something purely physical, but women rarely mean that. Go slow. Be gentle. Something tells me this woman is still healing from some pretty massive trauma in her past."

I nodded and looked down at the counter, bristling at Gavin's paternal tone. When had my brother become the expert on childhood trauma? The Gavin I knew five years ago would have encouraged me to fuck her out of my system, and the Gavin I knew just last year would have told me to run the other way.

But the Gavin standing in front of me now was

contemplative and empathetic. It was clear to me then more than ever how much his marriage to Emma had changed him.

In any other moment, I would have been impressed by my brother's insight. Right then, however? I was about ready to pop him in the eye.

"Right," I said, meeting Gavin's stern gaze with a cold look of my own. "I know all that. You weren't the only one with a rocky childhood, you know. I was there too."

Gavin raised his hands in surrender. "Not trying to start anything," he said, shaking his head. "Just want to make sure we're on the same page here."

I nodded and took another sip of my water. "So, what do you suggest?" I asked, ready to move on to more practical advice.

"First, there has to be a lot of conversation before you start slapping your private parts together. Start with goals with limits," Gavin said, walking around the island and taking a seat at one of the bar stools to my left. "You need to learn what's on her no-go list. Some women are perfectly fine getting fucked in the ass but won't let you kiss them on the mouth, so you need to ask. You two might not be interested in romance, but her pleasure will depend on how much trust you can build between the two of you."

I nodded, making a mental list of all the things I needed to do. I wasn't expecting there to be such an emphasis on actually having a conversation, but it made sense as Gavin explained it to me. "Thanks, man. What else?" I could see there was more he wanted to say.

"The conversation shouldn't stop there. During physical intimacy, you'll want to make sure there's a lot of communication. Get her to tell you how she's feeling, what she likes, what feels good."

I nodded. "Do we need to establish a safe word?"

He shook his head. "I don't think so. If it makes you feel more comfortable, you can, but generally, the words *no* or *stop* should suffice."

"Got it. Should I plan a proper date then?"

"That's a good place to start. It doesn't have to be romantic, but she should know she's valued. I could make you a reservation at the Union. The owner's a friend."

"No, I don't want to intimidate her," I said, remembering the blush that so easily spread across her cheeks and her perfect, ample chest. "Maybe a quiet dinner at home would be best. I could cook for her. It'd be intimate, that's for sure."

Gavin chuckled. "Cooper, you and I both know you can't cook. I'll send Emma over to help you. She'll make sure whatever you serve your date is edible."

I paused, unsure of how to respond. While the mention of Emma no longer sent a pang of sadness and regret shooting through my whole body, I hadn't talked to her since my stint in Florida, and part of me didn't want to see her again for the first time under these circumstances.

The more I thought about it, however, the better the idea sounded. It would be good to clear the air with her, and then I could finally patch up the old wound for good. That way, my focus could be solely on Corinne and her pleasure.

"Sure, Emma can help," I said. For once, I was grateful for my brother's unaffected nature.

"It's settled then." Gavin nodded. "Just know that if

you manage to catch your apartment on fire, even on Emma's watch, there's no way I'm paying for it," he said with a wink.

• • •

At work, I didn't press Corinne, and kept our relationship strictly professional. In the meantime, I did my best to make sure that my home felt welcoming and inviting.

Wednesday night, I called her and asked if she'd like to come to my place for dinner on Thursday—not a date night—and she agreed to come. Even in our five-minute conversation over the phone, she sounded nervous, so I was determined to take Gavin's advice and do everything in my power to make sure she felt safe and comfortable around me. I understood then that a solid foundation of trust would be the only way she would ever allow herself to surrender to the pleasure I wanted to give her.

My apartment wasn't a bachelor pad, per se, but it was clear that I didn't live with a woman. Huge TV, plush leather sofa, fully stocked bar—I didn't spend money on things like decorative pillows or complementary ottomans. I was concerned only with quality and function, which meant state-of-the-art appliances, the latest in high-definition technology, and the kind of furniture that was so well-made, it would last for generations after I was gone. I liked the way I lived, but I didn't want Corinne to feel timid or out of place in my home, so I did my best to soften my place's rough, industrial edges.

Once my apartment felt sufficiently non-threatening, I made a quick trip to the store to pick up the ingredients I needed for dinner that night. Normally, I relied on delivery services to leave my favorite meals on my doorstep, either ready to eat or in need of a mere half hour in the oven, so the grocery store was kind of new territory. Still, I had decided to cook for Corinne to make my home feel even more inviting, and I could only do that with fresh ingredients I'd picked out myself.

Gavin was right when he said I wasn't much of a cook, but he didn't know I'd taken a cooking class during a week-long vacation in Italy. The instructor was gorgeous, so I took the class three times, and while I failed to win the affections of the beautiful Italian culinary goddess, I did succeed in learning to make a killer lasagna from scratch. I didn't make the dish often—not even my brothers knew about my secret cooking skills—but the few times I chose to do so, it always paid off.

As I wandered through the aisles of the store, looking for fresh lasagna noodles and grass-fed beef, I went over Gavin's advice in my head. I knew that the moment Corinne stepped through the door into my home, it would take every ounce of willpower I had not to rip her clothes off then and there. The way her perfectly round ass filled out the little pencil skirts she wore hit me right behind the zipper, and part of me longed to skip all the talking and go straight to showing her how good I could make her feel.

Just as I started to imagine exactly what I wanted to do to Corinne, my thoughts were interrupted by my phone buzzing in my pocket. When I pulled it out, I was surprised to find Emma's name on my screen.

"Emma, hi, what's going on?"

"Cooper, where are you? I've been ringing your doorbell for five minutes now."

Fuck.

In all my preparations for my date with Corinne, I'd completely forgotten that Emma was coming over beforehand to help me cook. Now I looked like the asshole who no longer wanted her help.

"Shit. I'm sorry, Emma. You got there sooner than I expected. I'm just finishing up at the grocery store. I'll be back soon."

"Oh, that's fine. No problem. I'll be here."

I smiled. Even after everything that happened, Emma was still willing to jump in and help me.

"You can let yourself in. The spare's hiding in one of the potted plants."

"Right. Thanks, Coop. See you soon."

"See you soon."

I hung up and stood there for a moment, waiting for a wave of nervousness or sadness to wash over me. But I didn't feel anything. Had I actually forgotten that Emma was coming over?

This whole Corinne thing was really getting to me.

When I arrived back at my place, I found Emma in the kitchen, sipping from a bottle of water and obviously lost in a book she'd brought with her.

"I see you had no trouble finding the key," I said, causing Emma to jump up out of her seat.

"Jesus, Cooper, you scared me!" she cried, looking like she was ready to throw her book at me.

I laughed and raised my hands in surrender. "Sorry. I forgot how jumpy you are."

Emma smiled. "Yeah, me too," she said, her eyes meeting mine with the kind of softness and familiarity that used to make my heart pound and my cock perk up in interest.

But in that moment? I didn't feel anything but the ease and comfort that comes from visiting with an old friend.

Once we'd unpacked the groceries, I began to make my secret lasagna recipe—browning the mix of sausage and ground beef; mixing the ricotta with garlic, parmesan, and herbs; and heating up a jar of pasta sauce. If I'd really planned ahead, I would have made my own sauce from scratch, but I didn't want to push my luck.

Emma watched me quietly from the corner, her eyes wide. "Looks like you hardly need me at all," she said playfully, crossing her arms.

I laughed. "Gavin doesn't know everything about me, you know."

"Yeah, no kidding." Emma smiled, leaning back against the counter.

After I finished assembling the lasagna, I placed it deftly in the oven, where it needed to cook on low heat for an hour before I took off the top layer of foil to brown the cheese.

"So, you're cooking for your new assistant, Corinne, huh?" Emma asked with a grin.

Corinne. Just her name had an effect on me. "Yeah. She's . . . great."

"That's awfully nice of you."

I wasn't sure what to say, because I wasn't sure what the fuck I was doing, but I returned Emma's easy smile.

We stood there for a moment in silence, and I decided that then was as good a time as any.

"Why don't you take a seat in the living room. I think we should talk," I said, motioning to the couch.

She nodded and took a seat, and I joined her after washing my hands.

"Listen, Emma," I said, shifting to face her fully. "I want to apologize for the way I handled things. You were honest with me from the beginning about not knowing what you wanted . . . it was unfair of me to just go radio silent when things didn't go my way."

"No, Cooper, I'm the one who's sorry. I should've been more up front with you earlier on. That whole time of our lives was so . . . chaotic. I wasn't thinking clearly, and you were the one who ended up getting hurt. I'm so sorry about that, really. You were such a good friend to me through it all. It breaks my heart to think of how I hurt you."

It was good to hear the words come out of Emma's mouth, even if I already knew that she was too sweet to hold on to any malice. "I appreciate your apology, Emma, but really, there's nothing to apologize for. You followed your heart. And when I see how happy you and Gavin make each other, it's clear that you made the right decision."

"Thank you," she said, her brows scrunching together in sincerity. "I can't tell you how much that means to me."

"I mean it," I said, pausing before I added, "Although my brother can still be quite the ass every now and then."

Emma laughed. "There are some things not even true love can change."

I smiled and my thoughts immediately returned to Corinne. She was so timid around me, like a fragile little dove. I was curious about awakening the tiger inside her. Maybe Emma was right, and love couldn't fix everything.

Mind-blowing sex and a few killer orgasms, on the other hand?

I had a feeling those might do the trick.

Chapter Eight

Corinne

This was it. I was about to begin my first evening with Cooper—the man who offered me a no-strings-attached sexual relationship centered around my pleasure. The man who made me want to crush my lips to his one second, and run in the other direction the next. The man who also happened to be my boss.

Come on, Corinne, pull yourself together.

When I reached Cooper's front door, I paused to take a deep breath and center myself before knocking.

Why was I so nervous? This date was a sure thing. No unbearable small talk, no cringe-worthy oversharing, no awkward fumbling through whether he'd kiss me good night or not. The whole point of our arrangement was to make things between us as simple as possible. We took emotions right out of the equation. We were doing this for me, so I would finally know what kind of pleasure I'd been missing out on, and have the confidence to take charge of my sex life.

So, why did I feel so uncertain about what I was about to walk into?

I took another deep breath and adjusted the waistline of my skintight jeans. They weren't the most comfortable item of clothing I owned, but they sure made my ass look great—and I could use all the confidence in the world tonight. I'd paired them with a pale pink top that showed what I thought was a good amount of cleavage, though Mauve had commented to me once that if the neckline on it was any higher, I'd look like a nun. Still, I felt pretty, maybe even something close to sexy, and I was as ready as I'd ever be to get the festivities started.

I knocked and within moments, Cooper appeared. As he stood there, his tall frame taking up the entire doorway, I had to take a moment to regain my composure. In the office, Cooper always looked good. More relaxed than Gavin or Quinn, maybe, but his sleek button-downs made him look put together, even when he had his sleeves rolled up.

But tonight? He looked positively edible. If Cooper in the office was nice to look at, Cooper outside of work was freaking irresistible. He wore a pair of dark blue jeans and a gray Henley shirt with the top button undone, the soft fabric outlining the muscles on his arms and chest just enough to leave little to the imagination.

"You look exquisite." Cooper smiled, snapping me out of my trance. "Please, come in." He stepped to the side out of the doorway, giving me space to walk around him.

I smiled weakly and ducked through the door, my heart pounding in my chest. "You look nice too."

Standing in the entryway, I took a quick look around, silently marveling at how polished the whole place looked. While I wasn't a professional at home decoration, I could tell that Cooper had good taste. Leather, wood, granite . . . all his surfaces looked natural and expensive. I loved my little apartment, but I couldn't imagine living somewhere this nice and put together.

"Your home is beautiful," I said as Cooper closed the door and turned to face me.

"Thank you." He placed a hand lightly on the small of my back. "Dinner's almost ready. Can I get you a glass of wine?"

I felt my cheeks redden and struggled to keep myself from jumping at his touch.

You're safe here. He's only trying to make you feel comfortable.

"Wine would be great, thanks," I said and followed Cooper into the kitchen.

He poured us each a glass of red, and I was grateful for something to settle my nerves. From the kitchen, I could see that Cooper had set his dining room table for two, complete with a white tablecloth and a single candle waiting to be lit on a delicate candlestick. The gesture was sweet, but my stomach churned at the romantic implications.

Cooper peeked into the oven, smiled to himself, and pulled a dish out, placing it triumphantly on a hot pad on the counter.

"What are we having?" I took a sip of my wine, trying my best to be casual.

"Lasagna." He shot me a cheeky grin. "It's a recipe I learned a few years back on vacation in Italy."

I choked a little on my wine, doing my best to play it off as an innocent cough. "You cook?"

He smiled. "Not really. If I'm being honest, this is the only thing I can make. In fact, when I told Gavin I'd be cooking for you, he sent his wife, Emma, over to make sure I didn't burn the place down."

"You told Gavin I was coming over?"

My head started swimming with nervous thoughts about other people knowing. Who else had he told? Did everyone in the office know? Did they all think I was easy? Cooper was my boss, which meant this wasn't exactly appropriate.

"I mentioned it in passing, yeah," Cooper said casually, but I could tell from the weird look on his face that there was more to it.

I didn't want to pry, though, so I shrugged it off. We weren't here to bare our deep dark secrets. We were here to do the other thing that scared the living daylights out of me.

Opening myself up. *Literally.*

I took another long swallow of wine.

"Hungry?" he asked.

"Starving, actually."

Cooper served us each a generous portion of the lasagna, complete with a side salad and a thick slice of Italian bread. When we sat down to eat, he lit the single candle on the table. It was a little corny, but I could tell he was trying to be sweet, so I decided not to say anything about it.

As we began eating, our conversation moved easily over light and casual topics. We talked about living in the city, our favorite places to eat, our go-to coffee orders, things like that. Cooper was easy to talk to and seemed interested in what I had to say. I still couldn't tell if it was genuine or if he was just putting on a show so I'd feel more comfortable, but I tried not to think about it too much. Despite the butterflies still fluttering in my stomach, I was having a good time, and I wasn't about to let my personal anxieties get in the way of that.

"So, uh, I want to explain a little bit about the whole telling-Gavin thing," Cooper said, looking across the table at me.

"Okay," I said, my voice wavering a little. Part of me was dying to know what he'd told his brother, but another part of me wanted to pretend that what we were doing was a giant secret.

"Gavin and I have a bit of a . . . troubled history. You know his wife, Emma? She used to work for the company. Not as a regular escort, but as a personal escort that Gavin and I shared. It wasn't as creepy as it sounds—

we just wanted someone on hand so we'd always have a date for events. As you can imagine, things got complicated really fast. Gavin and I both ended up falling for her. And, uh, I guess it's clear how that love triangle ended." Cooper paused to take a sip of his wine. The look on his face was grim and remorseful.

Why was he telling me all this? I couldn't decide if I wanted to know more, or if I was ready to get out of this conversation before he expected me to share something equally personal. Before I had a chance to say anything, though, Cooper continued.

"I wanted you to know that I'm over it. Emma and I cleared the air earlier today when she came over to help me with the cooking. My feelings for her are purely friendly now. Or brotherly, I guess. We're in-laws, after all." Cooper smiled to himself, and I could see that he was being genuine.

"Well, thanks for telling me that, I guess," I said, fumbling over how to respond. "But you didn't have to share all that with me, you know. We don't have to dredge up our deepest darkest secrets, do we?" I silently prayed that he didn't expect me to reciprocate his sharing, even if it felt like he would be understanding of whatever I wanted to tell him.

Cooper smiled. "No, don't feel like you need to tell me anything. Not until you're ready."

I smiled back, thankful for his patience.

We chatted a little while longer before clearing our plates and doing the dishes together. I insisted on cleaning it all up myself because he had cooked, but Cooper refused to let me do the dishes alone. Once the kitchen was clean, we each poured ourselves another glass of wine and settled in on his plush leather couch.

I sat near him, but not too close. We talked about small things—television, music, and the like—before there was a brief lull in the conversation. Cooper cleared his throat and gave me a serious look.

"Tell me one thing no one knows about you," he said. It wasn't really a question, but it didn't feel like a command. He was trying to move us into a slightly deeper conversation, and it made my pulse thrum.

"I can't sleep without a white-noise machine," I said shyly, not daring to meet his gaze.

I could see the hint of a smile on his lips. He was silent for a beat before saying quietly, "Thank you for sharing."

I turned to face him, his green eyes piercing mine. I knew then that Cooper was unlike any other man I'd ever met. He was huge and handsome, had cooked me dinner, wanted to help me out of my shell, promised me orgasms, *and* was willing to supply me with orgasms. It was all a little overwhelming.

Cooper continued asking me questions, delving deeper into my preferences and limits, especially sexually. I told him that I wasn't interested in pain—no whips, no spanking, no being tied up. The last thing I wanted was to be humiliated. He listened intently, nodding along to everything I said. Once I was done explaining what I wasn't looking for in this *relationship*, he took my hand in his, his giant palm making mine look small in comparison.

"I promised that I will always make you feel cherished and safe and good. All I want is for you to feel the pleasure you've been denied," he said, looking intensely in my eyes.

I nodded and looked down at my hand in his. I didn't understand why Cooper was doing this, why he was so intent on making sure that I was okay. But I appreciated it.

A wave of emotion welled up inside me, a mixture of thankfulness, relief, and a hint of arousal. I brought my gaze back up to his, pausing briefly at his mouth. He leaned toward me, offering his lips for the taking. Ignoring the butterflies in my stomach, I leaned into him and pressed my lips to his, soft and gentle, allowing myself to get comfortable with the feel of his mouth on mine. We continued like that for a while, kissing slowly and softly, and it felt like he was coaxing me into more.

Whatever he was doing, one thing was clear to me.

It was working.

I relaxed into him, and we both shifted closer to each other, our hands wandering over each other's bodies. Cooper ran his fingertips gently across my back, down my side, and over my hip before beginning the whole motion again, and my skin felt electric under his touch. I pressed my hands against his chest, savoring the way his muscles rose and fell to the rhythm of his breathing. We were both breathing heavily, small gasps and moans escaping from my mouth every time his tongue wandered over to my neck or across my collarbone.

Warmth spread from between my legs to the ends of my entire body. I was wetter than I was the first time we kissed—and I didn't think that was possible. I could tell that Cooper was turned on too, but if I had to guess by how patient he was being, I would have said that he had no interest in going any further.

The need for more grew stronger inside me.

Was Cooper always this restrained? What about all those orgasms I was promised?

I kissed him harder and faster, moving my tongue more feverishly against his, and Cooper seemed to get the hint. Without skipping a beat, he placed his hand on my thigh, running it down to my knee before moving up between my legs. He touched me gently over my jeans, and I could feel that my panties were soaked through. I moaned at his touch, and his fingers moved deftly to my waist, unbuttoning my jeans and undoing the zipper. My heart pounded harder than ever, and even though I was nervous, no part of me wanted him to stop.

Within moments, Cooper moved his body over mine, peeling my jeans off and settling in between my legs. I moved my knees wider apart to make room for his massive frame as he began kissing the insides of my thighs. I threw my head back on the couch, my breathing ragged in anticipation of what I knew what was about to happen.

"Tell me this is okay, little dove," he murmured as his fingers slid under the waistband of my lace panties.

"Yes, please," I whispered.

He pulled my panties down, and I lifted my bottom so he could remove them completely.

The moment his tongue came into contact with my clit, I felt like my heart was going to explode. He licked slowly and purposefully over the length of my folds, and I couldn't contain the low moans that came out of me. As Cooper continued working his mouth over my sex, my entire body responded to him. My back arched and my moans were frequent—the pleasure overtook me in a way I never thought it could.

Without thinking, I reached for his head, running my fingers through his hair as my hips moved to the rhythm of his tongue. Within minutes, I felt an orgasm building inside me, and I could tell that Cooper felt it too. He lapped at my folds with more purpose than ever, coaxing me to climax, and when I came, it felt like my soul left my body. I melted into the couch, letting waves of pleasure wash over me until there was nothing left.

Cooper rose to his feet and sat down next to me, running his hand tenderly over my thigh. We sat there for a moment, our chests heaving, and suddenly, I became aware of how exposed I was. My jeans and panties were in a puddle on the floor, my nakedness fully on display. A wave of shame washed over me and I jumped to my feet, pulling up my pants and hastily buttoning them.

What have I just done?

I had to get out of there. *Now.*

"I, uh, I have to go," I said, looking frantically around the room to find my purse, my phone, my shoes. I gathered my things in a hurry, making a point not to look at Cooper. I could hear him saying something indistinct, but I wasn't listening. I didn't care what he had to say. All I knew was that I couldn't be around him anymore, that I needed to find somewhere else to be—and fast.

Before he could stop me, I ran out the door and closed it behind me, taking the elevator down and walking swiftly to my car.

The drive home was a blur, my mind racing with frantic, embarrassed thoughts. I couldn't believe that Cooper had just seen so much of my naked body, that I had let him do the things he did to me. No matter how good it had felt in the moment, I couldn't shake the shame that consumed me at the thought of myself on display for him, fully exposed on the couch he sat on every day.

When I got home, I immediately took a shower, still numb from my reaction to the intimacy Cooper and I had shared. It was too much—I knew that now. Even with how patient he had been in the moment, I felt like we had crossed a line, and I didn't know if I could ever look him in the eye again. As I did my best to scrub the shame off my skin, I could feel my heart pounding throughout my entire body.

I wasn't prepared for the level of intimacy and intensity that Cooper had to offer. I thought I'd wrapped my head around our arrangement, but I guess I'd pictured two people under the sheets in a dark room, not what had just happened where I'd been so exposed, so worshipped by his mouth. It was overwhelming.

One thought kept running through my mind, louder

and clearer than all the rest.

I never should have said yes to Cooper's offer.

Chapter Nine

Cooper

Heaven and hell, all wrapped up into one tidy evening.

I chugged my third cup of coffee, the second of which already had my stomach churning with acid. But there was no help for it. It had been a sleepless night, and I had a full day of work ahead of me. If only I could get Corinne out of my head for two fucking seconds, I'd be golden.

And if I could wipe away the memory of her running out of my apartment like her ass was on fire last night, I'd be extra golden.

Fuck.

The evening had started promising enough. At least, that's what I'd thought at the time. But the more I ran it over in my mind, the more I wasn't sure. Our agreement had been for no-strings sex, and what had I done?

I'd made it a date. Cooked her dinner, even. That was personal. More personal was my mouth all over her sweet pussy, tasting her like she was my last meal.

Though I was pretty sure it was my outpouring of information about Emma and Gavin that had pushed it all too far. I'd encouraged Corinne to share in kind and she'd offered me glimpses of her past, but I could see now in hindsight that I'd pushed too hard, too fast. Maybe she wasn't as willing to share her pain as I was.

It made sense. After all, it would be hard to work with a person after you'd bared your soul to them.

Then again, it was also hard to make love with someone who didn't know the first thing about you.

I'd struggled with these questions and more all night after she left. Thinking about the way she'd looked sitting across from me at dinner, and then the way she'd been in my arms later.

Which, of course, was the strangest thing of all.

If I'd put her off with my questions, why had she gone along with it so readily? Her kisses had been effortless, timid but curious, just like her demeanor. My sweet little dove. And when I'd dropped between her thighs and seen that perfect pink pussy waiting for me, she'd been so wet and ready that I'd had no doubt of what she wanted. I just wanted to ease her ache, to bring her to orgasm and hear her soft whimpers.

Even now, as I licked my lips, I could feel her heated skin. Could practically taste her as I remembered her bucking against me, her responsive little body moving with my every touch.

I let out a frustrated sigh and dumped my empty mug into the sink before glancing at the clock. This day wasn't going to go by any quicker with me just standing here like an idiot.

I snatched up my laptop bag and hustled out of the apartment. On a whim, and for the fiftieth time since I'd gotten out of bed, I reached into my pocket and checked my phone just in case . . .

But there were no text alerts, so I jammed it back into my pocket before slipping into my car and cruising toward work.

The time to make sense of everything before I saw her next was running out fast. But if I hadn't sorted things out overnight, it seemed unlikely that I was going to do it in the few minutes it took to get to midtown.

I could just ask her what had happened, I supposed . . . if she even bothered to come to work today. Or ever again.

Fuck.

Of all the scenarios I'd imagined, that was the one that worried me most. I sucked my bottom lip between my teeth and chewed, thinking hard. She couldn't—she wouldn't—give up this job just because of me. We paid too well for her to do that, and besides, it wasn't as though we'd actually slept together.

So I'd gone down on her. Lots of bosses had probably done that to their assistants, right?

I almost snort-laughed at the thought, imagining what Quinn would say to that.

Okay, so maybe not. Still, it wasn't the end of the world. If, after whatever had happened, she never wanted to see me again outside of work . . .

I shook my head at the sharp stab of discomfort in my gut as the acid there began to roil again.

No point in getting all worked up over something that might not even come to pass. I'd cross that bridge when I came to it. For now, I had to focus on looking like I hadn't spent last night tossing and turning, pining like a fifteen-year-old boy over the cute new girl at summer camp.

I climbed from my car after parking in my designated spot, and then hustled toward the wide, rotating doors that led to the offices of Forbidden Desires. With a steadying breath, I stepped inside the elevator just in time for my gaze to land on the woman who'd been the cause of my distraction all night.

The second I saw her, my cock swelled and my mouth watered with the memory of her sweet taste.

Shit.

I cleared my throat in the hope that I could keep my voice from dropping into that husky tone it did when I was turned on. "Corinne," I murmured, sidestepping as someone pushed into the elevator beside me, forcing me close enough to smell Corinne's delicate scent.

Her cheeks went pink and her throat worked for a second before she nodded in greeting. "Good morning, Cooper."

I glanced at the people surrounding us in the elevator. I wasn't about to put her on the spot in front of an audience, but I couldn't help myself entirely.

"How was your evening?" I asked, keeping my tone light.

She swiped a hand above her upper lip. When I realized it had broken out into fine beads of sweat, the coiling dread in my stomach instantly began to unwind.

Corinne could run, but she couldn't hide.

She had been just as affected by last night as I was. Maybe that was why she'd been afraid. This thing between us—whatever it was—was powerful. Overwhelming. I could understand the urge to back away.

The only question now was whether I should let her.

"My evening was fine. Just fine."

"Anything fun happen?" I asked innocently.

"Um, nope," she said, her tone shrill, and she shrugged. "Just hung out at home, mostly." She glanced from me to the corner of the elevator and rocked back and forth on her heels.

A second later, the metal doors slid open with a ding. A tall man in a blue blazer stepped out, leaving us alone with a severe-looking older woman.

"Me too," I said when the doors had closed again.

"Nothing interesting at all."

Corinne turned to face me, her eyes wide with something like confusion and possibly even hurt.

Damn it.

I was confused myself, but I certainly hadn't meant my teasing to make her feel bad.

She seemed like she wanted to say something when the elevator jolted to a stop again and the doors opened. The woman strode out, leaving the two of us alone. Corinne craned her neck, looking around with wide, desperate eyes, clearly considering getting out to hike the stairs the rest of the way, but before she could bolt, the doors closed again.

She leaned back against the metal handrail and gripped it for dear life. I could practically hear her counting the seconds until we reached our floor and were surrounded by people again.

"Corinne, look," I said, but she gave me a faint shake of the head.

"No. I really don't want to talk about it."

"Don't you think we should, though? We have to

work together, and this awkwardness is going to be evident to anyone looking on."

"We're almost to our floor, and I need to get my head together," she said in a rush. I could almost feel the desperation rolling off her. "Besides, anyone could get on, and this is private."

I paused. That was a fair enough point, but it didn't stop the curiosity burning its way up my throat. One question. Just one.

Why did you run?

"Come to my office after you've gotten your things settled. I want to make sure we're on solid ground. I promise, I won't pressure you for . . . anything. We need to clear the air, though. For both our sakes."

She nodded, though she refused to look at me.

And I wished like hell I knew what to make of that.

The doors dinged again, and she gripped her purse tighter against her as she made a beeline for her desk at a near sprint.

"Hey, good morning! Someone's ready to get to work," Alyssa teased, but Corinne just smiled weakly as she unpacked the few items in her bag and powered up her computer.

I exited the elevator more slowly, glancing around for any sign of my brothers before making my way to my own office and flicking on the lights.

The place was exactly as I'd left it, but it felt different somehow. Like something had changed in the hours I'd been gone.

I settled into my chair and turned on my computer before making a pot of coffee, staring at the clock as the sounds of boiling water and rising steam filled the air around me.

It wouldn't take long for Corinne to get her things in order. I knew that much. The real question was whether she'd have the courage to come in here at all.

When the coffee had finished percolating, I poured myself a mug and returned to my desk, opening a blank document to stare at, if only to pretend I was doing actual work. Instead, I contemplated writing down everything that had happened between Corinne and me—as if the factual recounting might show me something I couldn't see from my own subjective place in the story.

God, please don't let her quit.

The thought surfaced out of nowhere and was so strong that I nearly typed it out, but I restrained myself. It was just that she was fitting in so well here and catching on so fast. After everything that had happened with Sonja, we hadn't been sure we'd be able to find anyone who would meet the needs of the position, but with Corinne? It felt like we finally had the full package again. And with some training, I could see her moving into the still-vacant office manager role.

Sighing heavily, I gripped my fresh cup of coffee tighter and lifted it to my lips for a sip as I heard a gentle knock on my office door. A timid, familiar knock.

My pulse stuttered, and I straightened as I called out, "Come in."

Corinne stepped inside, entrancing me with her wavy hair, creamy skin, and lethal curves.

Gently, she closed the door behind her, and I took a moment to admire the way her sweater dress clung to her before she took a few more steps toward my desk and seated herself opposite me in one of my leather office chairs.

"Good morning again," I said, wishing I could lean in and taste that pretty mouth. Fighting the need to lift her onto my desk and test those petal-soft folds to see how quickly I could get her wet and panting for me.

No, Cooper. Bad Cooper.

I was like a child who needed my hand slapped.

"Good morning." She laced her fingers together and placed them primly on her knee before staring at her folded hands. "Y-you asked me earlier what I did last night." She lifted her chin and met my gaze. "Other than the time we spent together, I mostly just did a lot of thinking."

"Oh?" I said, trying not to jump out of my skin with impatience.

"Yes." She nodded. "I think I need to apologize to you, Cooper. I thought that I could do this ... arrangement, you know, with professional workdays and sexual encounters in our personal time, but I just can't."

Her words hit me like a fist to the solar plexus, and the room seemed to close in around me.

"So, you want to have the sex at work?" I tried for the feeble joke just to regain some sort of equilibrium, but her cool expression let me know instantly that I had blundered.

Seemed like it was getting to be a habit with her.

"I want to continue working together amicably and platonically. I'm sorry, but my decision is made. I don't want to do this."

Even as she spoke, though, she was shaking her head. Despite her strong words, her eyes were filled with doubt, which, in turn, filled me with confidence.

Slowly, I shook my head, encouraging her to maintain eye contact with me by sheer force of will. "No. I don't think that's true."

"Ex-excuse me?" she stuttered, the pulse in her neck throbbing like a butterfly trapped beneath the surface of that silky flesh.

I pushed myself to my feet, my sadness and insecurity fizzling away, leaving behind only confidence and thick, hot need. I rounded the corner of my desk until I was only inches away, towering over her.

"I think you're lying, Corinne. To me, but more importantly, to yourself. I think this is exactly what you want. In fact, I think you want it so much, it scared you."

Her cheeks went crimson as she shot to her feet, meeting me toe-to-toe. It didn't seem to matter to her that she was a good ten inches shorter than me, she straightened her shoulders, her posture stiff, ready to square off.

"That's ridiculous."

"Is it?" I cocked an eyebrow. "I felt how responsive you were in my arms, how much you wanted me. I can see your breath quickening right now as I get closer to you. Your nipples getting hard beneath that dress."

She quickly folded her arms over her chest, but it was too late. Like a shark scenting blood in the water, I knew the truth.

"You want me, Corinne, but you're afraid. That's why you ran. That's why you're trying to run now."

She shook her head, but I caught her chin and held her so her gaze met mine.

"Tell me you don't want to know what else we could do to together. Tell me you don't wonder what it would feel like."

She looked at me for a long moment, studying me, and then finally said, "I can't. I can't do that."

"You know I'm right."

"I do."

I released her and she took a step back.

"But," she said, "it's more complicated than it should be. There are things you don't know. Things that I need to work through. I'm trying to save you from yourself here," she said with a short, humorless laugh. "Cooper, I'm a mess. I'm high-maintenance and I'm not an idiot. I know you could have any woman you want."

I took another step toward her, closing the space between us as I wrapped my hand around her waist. "The only woman I want is you, dove."

Gently, I pulled her toward me, breathing in her perfume as she came closer, and then, finally, savoring the sweet heat of her lips on mine. The kiss started so slowly, it wasn't even a kiss—just two people standing inches apart, our lips touching as soft breaths passed between us.

But then her lips parted, and I could have groaned at her invitation, but I didn't. Instead, I pressed forward, licking her lower lip. When her tongue swept out to greet me, I groaned with both relief and desire. I stepped forward, pressing her back until she was flush against the door as I matched her tongue stroke for stroke. We sank into each other, fitting together like two pieces of a puzzle. It was perfection.

The hammer of desire came down hard, and all the pent-up need and frustration of the past few days hit me at once. The blood rushed from my head downward as I ground against her, letting her low, throaty moans fill my senses.

Yes. This was what I wanted more than I'd wanted anything I could remember.

Her hand slid up between us to grip the cotton of my shirt, anchoring me closer even as her hips pulsed restlessly against me.

This was good. So good that I wasn't about to fuck it all up by having us get caught screwing around at work and sending her running again.

Regretfully, I pulled away. It took every ounce of strength I had not to lock the door, drag her over to my desk, and—

"Right." She gasped, her hand fluttering to her heaving chest. "We're at work. Good call."

We stared at each other for a long moment, and I leaned in to press my forehead against hers. Something about this woman—the feel of her, the taste of her, just her general presence—made me want to know her. To have her completely as my own.

I pressed one last gentle kiss to her lips and dropped my voice to a whisper. "Someday, when I've earned it, will you tell me what happened? Why you're still single? Why you're so timid?"

She searched my gaze, though she didn't cower or look away. Instead, she gave me the briefest of nods. "Not now, Cooper. Not yet."

"I know about the orphanage," I said softly. "Does it have something to do with that?"

She nodded, the sadness in her eyes making me want to snatch the question back. "Yes, but that's not all of it. There's . . . more."

I nodded. "Okay, then I won't push you. Just know that I'm a great listener and I care, Corinne. More than you know."

She wet her lips and smoothed a hand over her dress as I stepped back. She closed her fingers over the doorknob, but before she twisted it open, she turned and met my gaze again.

Unwavering, she nodded once. "I care too, Cooper. Just so you know."

She flung the door open, and just like that, she was gone, leaving me staring after her.

Today hadn't been without its bumps, but damn it, she wanted me as much as I wanted her. And more than that?

She cared.

A slow grin spread over my face as I made my way to my desk, suddenly full of energy.

Chapter Ten

Corinne

This was a bad idea.

Though, of course, it hadn't seemed that way when I'd agreed to do it.

Leaving Cooper's office with my head swimming from that mouth of his, I wandered back to my desk and stared blankly at my computer screen for a long time, still savoring the heat of his touch on my skin. He was maddeningly sexy—a great kisser—and so freaking intuitive, he seemed to know exactly what I was thinking and feeling before I did.

I could feel Alyssa watching me from the corner of her eye, could tell that she was wondering what had happened while I was in Cooper's office. But being the consummate professional she was, she'd never ask me about that during work hours.

Instead, she invited me to lunch, holding in her curiosity as we grabbed our purses and headed to the food court on the bottom floor of the building.

The second we stepped into the elevator, though?

The inquisition began.

"Have you gotten a single thing done since you talked to Cooper this morning?" she asked, a knowing smile painted on her lips.

"What? No. I mean, yes. Of course I have."

"Ooh, you're all frazzled. That's a good sign. Something happened," Alyssa cooed with glee.

I rolled my eyes and tried to make a poker face, which I was pretty sure I didn't have in my repertoire. "Don't be silly."

The elevator chimed as the doors slid open, and Alyssa switched the subject to ask which of the food stalls we should hit. When we'd finally decided on sandwiches and had gotten our food, I sighed with relief. It was only once we were seated that I realized the lull had just been a ruse to lure me into a false sense of security until she could strike again.

She held her tuna sandwich and stared at me expectantly.

"What?" I asked.

"So." She wrinkled her nose. "Cooper."

"God, that again?"

"Yes, that again. Is he a good kisser?"

"What?" I practically gasped. Was I really that obvious?

"You walk out of his office all flushed and dazed, and I'm supposed to think—what? That he gave you a glowing performance review?" She chomped on her sandwich, then flicked me a sassy look. "Spill."

"You're being silly. I barely know Cooper."

"That doesn't mean that you can't bone down." Alyssa shrugged.

"Ew, God. Is that what people call it nowadays?"

"So, you're saying you think it would be gross to have sex with him?" Alyssa cocked an eyebrow.

"I never said that. I'm objecting to the phrase 'bone down.' It's just so wrong, Alyssa."

"Right. Prude." She sighed. "So, you're really not going to tell me anything?"

"There's nothing to tell." I pursed my lips, then thinking hard, added, "Though, it might be nice to know a little more about him."

"You don't want to tell me what's up between the two of you, but want intel from me?" she said with a snort. "Like what?"

"I don't know. Just stuff about him, I guess. General sort of stuff." I shrugged, toying with my food.

Alyssa shook her head. "You're barking up the wrong tree there. I don't know a whole lot about any of them except for Gavin, and even he's a mystery to me sometimes. The person to talk to is Emma."

"Emma?" The memory of everything Cooper had told me flooded back, and my stomach roiled with the thought of seeing the other woman, let alone talking to her.

God, did he still think about her? Want her? He'd said he didn't, but maybe that was just a line.

I set my sandwich down, suddenly no longer hungry.

"She knows everything about all of them, and I hear through the grapevine that she's a lightweight. Get a couple drinks in her, and I bet she'll spill everything she knows."

I wrinkled my nose. "That seems sort of wicked and conniving, don't you think?"

Alyssa quirked her mouth to the side. "I don't know. As wicked as not telling your best work friend why you suddenly want to know all about Cooper?"

"Alyssa," I pleaded. "Look, I promise I'll tell you if and when there's something to tell. I swear, we haven't," I looked around and dropped my voice to a whisper, "boned down yet or anything, okay?"

"Fine, fine," she said with a roll of her eyes. "I'll set it up. We'll have a girls' night, and you can ask Emma everything you want in any state of soberness you choose. But if you guys do it, I'm the first to know. Deal?"

"I . . . I guess it would be good to get out for a while and hang with some girls," I said, though I couldn't deny the rush of excitement surging through my veins. Jeez, first a happy hour and now a girls' night. My social calendar was suddenly exploding.

"Sure, that's why you want to go." Alyssa laughed and took another bite of her sandwich. After securing my promise to share if and when Cooper and I ever did the deed, she moved on to telling me about a to-die-for pair of pumps she'd picked up at Macy's for a steal, and the matter seemed closed.

• • •

And that's how I'd ended up here that same evening, waiting on my doorstep for Alyssa's car and thinking over every last detail of what Cooper had told me about Emma.

The idea that he had had feelings for her in the past? It shouldn't have bothered me, especially when we had no expectations in our own relationship, but I couldn't help feeling ... jealous. It was so stupid, but it was there—deep in my gut and impossible to ignore.

When Emma and Alyssa finally did arrive, I felt even more so. I was a whole foot down on the attractiveness totem pole. Emma was slim with perfect plum-sized breasts, and her formfitting dress did nothing to hide the fact that her body was one worth showing off. There wasn't an ounce of fat anywhere on her. I tugged on my silk blouse, hyper-aware of how these skinny jeans showed off every curve and the thickness of my thighs. As I climbed into the backseat, I forced a smile I very much didn't feel.

I'd never been so aware of my ample curves in my life, and as I glanced at her again, I wondered how it was possible Cooper had ever looked at me twice compared to her.

"Hey!" Emma said, her smile appearing genuine. "This was a fun idea. I was so glad when Alyssa called me. So, we're going to this place Gavin took me a couple of months ago. It's a little loud, but the bands are always good."

"Sounds great," I said.

"I hope you don't want any quality time with me then, because I will be dancing," Alyssa said from the driver's seat.

Emma and I grinned at her, and together we chatted casually about work and how I was adjusting to my new job. Emma was really nice, and by the time we got to the bar, I was feeling like a royal brat for this plan to use her to get information on Cooper.

As Alyssa handed over her keys to a valet, I vowed to reassess my reasons for being here. I needed to let go of the idea that I was vetting the competition or using her to get information. This was going to be a fun girls' night, and that was that. But if Cooper came up in conversation . . .

Jeez, Corinne. Play nice. She's not the competition. Emma chose his brother—and she's happily married now.

Shutting those thoughts down, I followed Alyssa and Emma to a table near the back of the club.

"We need something strong to get us started," Alyssa announced, thumbing the drink menu. "A round of cosmopolitans and some shots of tequila too, please," Alyssa called to the waitress before offering me a not-so-sly wink. Emma made no motion to protest, and when the waitress returned, we all downed our shots with a toast to Forbidden Desires.

Then, drink in hand, Alyssa flitted off onto the dance floor, bobbing her head along with the music as she moved. I laughed as she nearly tripped, but then Emma's voice caught my attention.

"Alyssa tells me you're curious about Coop," she said, a tiny smile curving her perfect lips.

I froze with my martini glass halfway to my mouth and winced. "Alyssa has a big mouth."

Emma laughed. "Not when it matters, usually. Is

there something going on between you and Cooper?"

She didn't seem angry or annoyed in the least. Just curious, and my nerves settled some. As irritated as I was at Alyssa for blowing my cover, I had to admit this felt better. Less sneaky.

I shook my head. I had no idea how much to tell Emma. The truth seemed like too much. I'd just met her. "Alyssa thinks there is. She's just trying to help."

Emma shot me an affectionate glance. "It's okay, Corinne. You can trust me. I won't try to cause any trouble for you. At work or otherwise, with Cooper."

"Thank you."

My gaze wandered to Alyssa, who had now found someone to bob alongside her to the beat.

"So, what do you want to know about Coop?" Emma asked, sipping her drink tentatively.

I shrugged. "I'm not really sure," I said honestly. *Everything* hardly seemed like a good response. "What should I know?"

"Well, if you're asking because he's your boss, I would say you need to know that he loves his company.

And for as awful as the woman was who did your job before, she was very good at it. They'll likely be watching you closely to make sure you stack up."

I considered this, then took a sip of my drink for courage. "And what if I was asking about him not as my boss? More like . . . as a man?"

Emma pursed her lips and seemed to consider that for a long moment. "That's a tougher question. He loves and he loves hard. He's loyal and sweet. I think he wants what he never got growing up."

The "loves hard" part stung, but I refused to dwell on that part. If Cooper said whatever he and Emma had was over, I chose to believe him. I was more interested in the latter part.

"What do you mean by that? What didn't he get growing up?"

She shifted in her seat, looking a little uncomfortable now. "Gavin doesn't like people to know about their story, so I typically don't tell it."

"And Cooper? How does he feel?" I asked.

Emma sighed. "He's always been more open than the other two brothers. And if you're asking about him as a man, I'm going to assume it's because you care about him."

She considered her drink for a long minute, then looked me squarely in the eye.

"I think the best I can say is that they were raised in a tough situation in a rough neighborhood. Their mom spent her time with unsavory people, and she had an equally unsavory job. That's shaped all of them in its own way. But at the end of the day? They all want to protect the people they care about. And Cooper, most of all, wants the kind of love between a man and a woman he never got to witness as a child."

A knife slipped between my ribs at her words, then twisted as I noted the way her eyes softened as she spoke about him. It might be over, but damn it, she loved him. Maybe not in the way he'd wanted her to, but she did love him, even if it was now only a brotherly love. I would have to deal with that, even if Cooper and I were only going to be lovers for a short while.

More than that, though, I had to deal with the fact that this woman knew him in a way I didn't. They shared a bond that he and I didn't. And suddenly, I wanted that.

Desperately.

"The more time you spend with him, the more he'll show himself to you. He's an easy guy to like." Emma smiled.

"He is. Thanks."

I sipped my drink again, then shook my head to clear it. She'd given me a lot to think about. Too much, maybe. But what her words had convinced me of was that whatever I felt for Cooper was worth exploring.

"What do you say we dance?" I said, desperate for an escape from all the heavy thinking I had ahead of me.

Together we joined Alyssa on the dance floor, and I learned the lyrics to every song the band played as Alyssa shouted them in my ear. As the night progressed, one shot turned to two, and then three.

By the time midnight rolled around, I was finally feeling less like I wanted to fall on a sharp object every time I looked at Emma, but even if I did? I doubted I would feel any pain.

I was swaying back and forth even as the band took a break, and when we found our table again, the euphoria of my drunkenness shifted from mellow to reckless.

Feeling more certain by the second, I picked up my phone and stared at it for a second before doing the thing I knew I'd probably regret.

I drunk-dialed Cooper.

He answered, his voice tight with worry. "Hey, are you okay? It's late."

"Fine, fine. C-can you pick me up, though? I think I drank too much, and I want to go home but I don't want to ruin the girls' night."

"Of course. Where are you?" he replied without hesitation.

I told him the name of the bar, and I heard rustling in the background. Had he been in bed?

"Stay right there. I'll find you," he said and clicked off a second later.

When I returned to the table, Emma and Alyssa had three glasses of water waiting for us.

"Here you go," Alyssa said. "We're gonna have one last dance and then head home. You cool with that?"

I shook my head. "No, no, I called a ride. But thank you."

Emma gave me a wobbly thumbs-up. "We'll wait with you until they get here."

"No, go ahead. You guys dance. I swear I'm fine," I said, and though I had to assure them roughly twenty more times, they eventually left just in time for Cooper to text me that he was waiting outside.

I recalled getting to my feet and making it to the sidewalk, and then a strong pair of arms closing around me.

And after that? It was all blackness.

• • •

Morning came in like a wrecking ball, pounding against my skull, demanding entry.

I cracked my eyes open to find I was still fully dressed and now surrounded by a sea of white. The down comforter and feather pillows surrounding me were luxurious and inviting.

In the distance, I heard the sizzle of something on a stove, and I forced myself to find my bearings, despite the fact that I felt like I was moving underwater. When I finally got to my feet, I stepped through the bedroom door to find Cooper at the stove in his light blue pajama bottoms, cracking an egg into a hot skillet.

"Good morning. How are you feeling?" He grinned at me as I slipped into a chair at the breakfast bar in his kitchen.

I forced myself to look away from his glorious body—because, holy shit, my boss had a six-pack and the sexiest muscled chest I'd ever seen outside of one of those men's fitness magazines—and scrubbed a hand over my face.

"Not great," I confessed with a pained chuckle. "Should I be embarrassed about anything I said or did last night?"

"Well, you told me my bed head looked cute, and patted my butt. Other than that, though? You passed out the second you got in my car. I carried you in and put you to bed. That was about it."

I groaned. "I'm sorry. God, I didn't realize I'd drank so much."

Cooper shrugged. "It's not a big deal, Corinne. I was happy to come pick you up."

Suddenly realizing things felt freer, I looked down at

myself, noticing for the first time my lack of a bra. "Um." I crossed my arms over my chest. "What happened to my bra?"

Cooper let out a chuckle, his gaze raking over me. "Oh yeah. I forgot about that." A smile tilted up the corners of his mouth. "When I laid you down in bed, you tugged at the straps like you were uncomfortable, so I removed it. Women don't usually sleep in them, right?"

I swallowed. "Oh. That's . . ." *Awkward.*

"Trust me, it was no problem at all. And I didn't even steal a peek."

I pursed my lips. "Aren't you a saint."

"Fuck yes, I am. You're so sexy, Corinne." His voice went husky as he watched me. "All those curves. You're stunning."

My gaze focused on the floor, I mumbled something of a disagreement. I was so not, but I didn't want to argue with him. "Thank you again for last night, but you don't have to babysit me," I said, rising to my feet. "Let me get out of your hair so you can—"

"No, not before you get some food in you," he said, shaking his head.

Another panicked thought crossed my mind, and I groaned. "No, really, my roommate is probably a wreck with worry. I always come home, and I didn't even call. I have to go."

Cooper shrugged. "So, call her now."

"Him," I said as I stood. "And I can't. My phone is dead."

"Him?" Cooper flipped the egg and then turned to face me. "You have a male roommate?"

"Yes." I tried to sound as casual as possible despite the fact that my stomach felt like it was going to rebel. That was probably something I should have divulged before now, but mentioning it brought with it a whole other can of worms.

"So . . . are you sleeping with him?" Cooper asked, his voice deceptively soft.

"What? No." I frowned, shaking my throbbing head.

"I had to ask," he said with a clipped nod, the concern on his face clearing. "But good. I trust you. And while we're involved, I want you to know you can trust me too. No fucking unless it's between you and me.

Deal?"

I refused to meet his gaze and searched for my purse, which I found hanging on the back of one of the high-backed chairs. "I just need to get home. Can we talk about this later?"

His face tensed again as he stared at me. "Do you have a history with this guy or something?"

I let out a long sigh. "Will you just please tell me where my shoes are?"

Cooper frowned. "Foot of the bed."

"Great. Thanks."

After I slipped into my bra and gathered my shoes, Cooper plated his eggs, leaving them to grow cold while he called me a car.

"Thank you again. And I'm really sorry for bothering you last night."

He nodded, watching me warily. "You didn't bother me."

I'd just gotten things back on a good footing with him the day before, and now, less than twenty-four hours later, here I was running again. Like a child.

But even that shameful thought didn't stop me as I slid on my shoes and bolted out the door.

Chapter Eleven

Cooper

In spite of everything that had happened last night and how it had ended, I couldn't bring myself not to message Corinne. From the second she'd hurried out my door early that morning, my mind had focused on nothing else.

Of course, I thought of her with her roommate—her so-called platonic friend. But it was more than that. In fact, whatever jealousy I felt was practically infinitesimal compared to my own curiosity.

What was Corinne like when she was out, partying with friends? What had her night been like? And most of all, why had I been the person she called—not another coworker or a friend, but me?

She was running scared, for sure. But I'd been the person she'd wanted when her guard was down. That had to matter. And there was no question that I couldn't give up so easily.

There was something about this girl that made me wonder about her in ways I'd never thought of anyone else. And so, when it finally became too much, I picked up the phone and tapped out a quick text.

> *What are you doing tonight?*

The reply came back a few minutes later.

> *Not sure.*

I considered the reply, and while it definitely wasn't super encouraging, she could have just said she had plans.

> *The museum downtown is having a zombie exhibit. They're doing a movie marathon there too. Want to go?*

I stared at the phone waiting for her reply. After the way she'd stormed out of my place like her ass was on fire this morning, I was afraid some part of me already knew the answer and just didn't want to accept it—that it was all over before it had even begun. But to my surprise, she messaged me back.

> *It's not a date, right?*

I smiled before typing out my reply.

> *Of course not. Do you really think I'd take a woman to a zombie display on a first date?*

Her reply came almost instantly

> *Good point. Okay, meet you there.*

I blinked and shoved the phone in my pocket, trying not to grin like an idiot, even though nobody was around to judge. Still, this felt like the start of something, the chance to make up for pushing too hard a couple of nights ago. To take it slower and chip away at the carefully constructed walls around the true Corinne.

The more I thought about her, the more I realized I only knew her in fragments—like shattered glass around a faded picture. There were sharp edges to her that would need to be navigated carefully, but if I could put it all together? I couldn't even begin to describe how satisfying that would feel.

I frittered away the rest of the afternoon, but when the time to leave finally came, I left full of anticipation as I made my way to the gallery. And even though I arrived ten minutes early just in case, I found Corinne standing outside, looking at the black-and-white posters of zombie movies from the 1960s.

Her purple skirt fluttered around her knees as she turned to face me, her hair swept along with the strong pull of the breeze. For a second, I wondered if it would be awkward after this morning. But then she smiled, and it was all I could do not to close the space between us and kiss her hello.

Fisting my hands in my pockets instead, I said, "Hey there. You look beautiful."

And she did. In her full skirt and short-sleeved white shirt and matching flats, she was adorably sweet and pure.

And don't forget it, Coop.

"Thanks." Her cheeks flushed a pretty pink. "You know, I was actually a little surprised you messaged me. Because of, well, the way I was this morning."

"It's in the past," I said to reassure her. "Really."

She nodded, though there was still a slight air of hesitation in her glance. "I'm really sorry for bugging you last night. I'm not usually a huge drinker like that, and it got out of hand. Thanks for picking me up."

"Anytime. Really," I said, my tone solemn, making sure she knew I meant it.

Her lips tipped into a relieved smile. "I appreciate it, Cooper. Let's head in, okay?"

She stuffed her hands in the pockets of her skirt and I followed, opening the wide glass museum doors for her to step inside. As we walked in, I stopped at the ticket counter and purchased our tickets.

"Thank you, but it's still not a date." Corinne said.

"Definitely not a date." I nodded in agreement. "Have you been here before?"

She smiled and nodded.

It wasn't an exotic or strange place to go, but I was desperate to get her talking about something—anything that might tell me more about her.

"I came on a school trip once," she said. "When I was young. One of my first placements."

"Placements?" I asked, the back of my neck tensing. "Like what? A foster family?"

Her lips thinned, but she nodded again. "The family lived in this school district, and I came with my class."

I wanted to wipe the pain in her expression away, hold her and tell her that I understood that kind of pain. Had lived through it. But instead, I focused on listening. I'd wanted her to talk to me. To open up. Now that she was, I wasn't about to fuck it up.

"Did you like it there?"

"In the city or with the family?" she asked.

I considered this, leading her into the next room of displays. "Not sure. Both?"

"They were fine. I was with them for the better part of a year. Lots of kids there, though. More a halfway house than a home."

"That sounds tough," I said softly.

"I'm sorry. I'm sure this is all incredibly riveting for you." She gave me a shy smile.

"I think you're wrong about that. I want to know everything you want to tell me," I admitted as we circled the room.

She looked a little surprised, and then chuckled. "Maybe another time. It's not all that exciting."

We stopped to survey a portrait of the cast of *The Walking Dead*, but as I scanned the photo, I got the impression Corinne was distracted, that something else was on her mind.

"You okay?" I asked.

"Yeah. It's nothing." She shrugged.

"It's not nothing. You have a look on your face."

"Then my face is lying," she said teasingly, but it came out sounding hollow.

I didn't say anything else, but I also didn't look away.

Finally, she sighed. "Fine. Well, I was just thinking with all this talk about my childhood . . ." She shook her head. "It's stupid."

"Come on, spit it out. I promise I won't laugh."

"I'm not worried about you laughing," she said. "I was just . . . well, I went out with Alyssa and Emma last night, and Emma mentioned that you had a rough childhood too. I was sort of curious."

"She just mentioned that out of thin air, huh?" I raised my eyebrows, and Corinne glanced away.

"I may have asked about you, so I guess that's the other reason I'm telling you about it. I feel a little bad for asking her, so I wanted to fess up."

"I see." I rocked back on my heels and then took another step toward her, strangely relieved that I wasn't the only one in this weird relationship who wanted to know more about the other. The real, grimy, gritty stuff that mattered.

"And what is it you want to know about my childhood?" I asked carefully.

"I'm not sure. What do you want to tell me?"

"How about we trade? A detail for a detail," I offered, feeling less restrained now that she'd been the one to broach the subject.

Corinne surveyed me warily, then finally nodded her head. "But no questions. Just fact for fact. Deal?"

The fear in her eyes was real and deep enough that it made my muscles tense with the caveman desire to find a time machine, go back twenty years, and tear somebody's head off for putting that haunted look on her face. But I stuffed that feeling down and focused on present Corinne, the one standing in front of me, wanting to get to know me. The *real* me.

"Deal," I said. "Rock, paper, scissors to determine who goes first?"

Her full lips twitched into a grin, and then we counted to three and drew our weapons. Rock for me, scissors for her.

Excellent.

"Best two out of three?"

"Nope." I shook my head. "I won fair and square."

She groaned. "Okay, fine. Um ..." She rubbed absently at her chin as we strolled slowly around the museum. "When I was about ten, I lived with a family of all girls, and on Friday nights, we watched movies but they were always starring Shirley Temple. We were all too old for them, but the foster parents insisted on showing them, regardless of the fact that we wanted to watch Mary Kate and Ashley movies."

"Sounds like a drag."

She shrugged. "Actually, I have a weird appreciation for them now."

"What's your favorite?"

"*The Little Princess*," she said softly.

It would be. A story of an orphaned girl who finds out that not only was she wealthy all along, but that her father was still alive. A fairy tale, if there ever was one.

"I've seen it. Good choice," I said.

She seemed to shake off the bittersweet memory and smiled up at me expectantly. "Okay, fair is fair. Now, it's your turn."

"Fine." I thought hard, wanting to offer something that felt personal, like a shared piece of myself, but also a little lighthearted like hers to ease us both into it. One false move, and I knew our little Q&A was over. I had to tread lightly. "My mother was rather eccentric, and when I was young, too young to really speak up, she used to dress me up and dance around our apartment with me. My brothers were both too big to go along with it, and they still tease me about it."

Corinne's eyes went wide. "Please tell me there are pictures."

Fact was, there weren't pictures of much from our childhood, thank God. There hadn't been money to waste on a camera, but I kept that to myself.

"None that have survived to see the light of day," I said. "Now, let's try a little more serious one this time."

She chewed on her bottom lip, studying me again with those soulful eyes of hers. "Something serious? Well, once, when I was probably in middle school, I got expelled."

"What? Why?" Looking at her now, I couldn't think

of anyone less likely to get herself into trouble.

"I was going to school here, right outside of Boston, and I skipped out on a field trip."

"What do you mean?"

She twirled an errant strand of hair, glancing toward the yellow brick road that led into the next room. "I got sick of the museums, and I wanted to be on my own. Most of my foster homes always had so many kids. I was always surrounded by people. I was tired of it, so I thought I would just live in Boston and see where it took me. They found me about three days later when the police picked me up for stealing from a food cart."

"Jesus." I scrubbed a hand through my hair as I imagined a younger, more naive Corinne on the streets alone. It made my blood run cold. "That was brave."

She shrugged. "Or stupid. Whichever. Now, what about you?"

"I'll tell you, but you have to promise it's not going to change anything between us. All this stuff is in our past, right?" I said.

She nodded warily.

She'd dug deep and had told me something very personal, and it was time to return the favor.

I blew out a sigh and bit the bullet. "The reason I was always surrounded by women was because my mom worked as a prostitute when I was young. My brothers and I protected her and, you know . . ." I shrugged and tried to keep my expression blank. "That was just how our lives were for a while."

Corinne considered me, but her expression didn't crumple with pity or disbelief. Instead, she simply said, "I'm sorry. That's a hard road."

"It was. But I'm the man I am today for it. Just like your past made you who you are."

"Right." She nodded, then strolled into the next room. She hadn't freaked out but she had definitely gotten quiet, and I knew our game of twenty questions had suffered an early demise.

Things felt . . . good between us, though. Easy. Right.

For a little while, we looked at each of the exhibits, and soon, the conversation began to flow again as we discussed movie magic before we made it to the movie viewing area. Tonight was *Night of the Living Dead*, and

Corinne admitted she'd never seen it.

As the classic film played, I watched her get sucked into the story, her eyes wide. When a zombie lurched at a young woman in a cemetery, Corinne clutched my bicep, which I didn't hate at all.

"You liked it?" I asked when the film was over.

She nodded. "Very much."

"Still not as good as Shirley Temple, though?" I teased.

She grinned. "Never."

The lights in the little room came up, and as people shuffled out around us, we stayed in place, watching them go. I could feel the tension rolling off her, and wondered if hers stemmed from anticipation, like mine, or if she was trying to figure out how to run again.

Only one way to find out.

"The museum is about to close. Come back to my place so we can continue our not-a-date?"

I thought I knew her answer before she said it. There was a wariness in her eyes, a caution. But just as before, she surprised me by looking me straight in the eye.

"Sure. Let's go."

Chapter Twelve

Corinne

Cooper had been nothing but a gentleman so far, and I'd had a nice time. So, why was my belly suddenly swamped with nerves? He'd promised me this wasn't a date, and I'd believed him, stupidly at the time.

Now I knew there was something hot stirring between us, and I totally didn't want to avoid it any longer.

When we arrived at his place, I noticed more details than I had before. The first time I'd been here, I'd been so nervous, and then the second was after I'd drank enough to intoxicate a small village. This time I could actually appreciate the clean, masculine lines of his penthouse with its open floor plan, soft gray wood floors, and cozy leather furniture. It also smelled faintly like Cooper—a mix of honey and leather.

"You have a lovely home," I murmured as he led me farther inside, past the kitchen and into the living room.

He gestured for me to have a seat. Remembering

what we'd done on this sofa a couple of nights ago sent a small ripple of pleasure through me. Jeez, had he needed to sanitize it afterward? I'd practically run out of here like my ass was on fire.

I took a deep breath and lowered myself to the couch.

"Is everything okay?" he asked.

I nodded, feeling slightly nervous, and I wasn't even sure why or how to put into words what I was feeling. I'd steeled myself a long time ago, convinced I couldn't have something like this. A fling. A casual affair. And yet here I was, with this gorgeous, sexy man who made me want all that and more.

Cooper placed his hand on my jaw and drew me closer, bringing his lips down to mine. "Thank you for this," he said against my lips.

"For what?" I hadn't done anything.

He shrugged, placing one soft kiss against my mouth. "For coming out with me. For being here."

That was when I suddenly realized it. Maybe us exploring this little affair was helping him as much as it was helping me. He'd admitted he'd been heartbroken before we met. I didn't know why it had never occurred to me before, but now it made sense. Cooper needed this distraction as badly as I did.

I placed my hands on his chest, not to push him away but to show him that I was here, right here with him in this moment.

"Kiss me, Coop," I whispered.

"Gladly." He smiled briefly and then his mouth crashed against mine, hot and hungry for me.

We kissed forever, until the space between my legs had grown wet and so achy, I could have screamed. I'd heard of going slow, but this was ridiculous. He was so strong, so deliciously male. God, I'd never wanted anything more.

As if sensing my need for more, Cooper broke away from the kiss and lifted my shirt from over my head, dropping it to the floor while his eyes feasted on my ample cleavage.

He placed a kiss on the top of each breast, and discreetly adjusted his erection. I swallowed a wave of nerves as his right hand traveled under my skirt.

With his fingers in my panties, Cooper paused with his mouth hovering inches from mine. "I want to make you feel good."

"You are," I said on a sob.

"I want to make you come," he whispered.

"Yes."

His fingers moved in slow, lazy circles, drawing out my pleasure, making my hips rock to get closer. "Tell me what you want, little dove."

I swallowed, my muscles tensing as his finger teased my opening, but didn't penetrate.

"It's late, and I . . ." God, my excuses sounded hollow, even to my own ears. "I should probably get going."

Cooper pulled his hand from my panties and sucked on his fingers. It was so sensual, so erotic. The idea that he wanted to savor me sent a thrill through me. "You taste so fucking good."

I watched him in stunned fascination. He was so open, so sexual—and it all came so easily to him. I admired him for that. What courage, what strength. I couldn't imagine putting it all out there, saying those dirty words without feeling totally self-conscious.

"You sure there's nothing that you want, beautiful?" His voice was rich and low.

It was now or never. My heartbeat was pulsing low in my groin, and I wanted him. Wanted him more than I'd ever wanted anything. *Speak up, Corinne.*

"Last time . . ." I huffed out a breath. "I liked what you did last time."

A slow, devilish grin spread over Cooper's mouth. "Thank fuck. I've wanted to bury my face in your pussy since I first saw you outside the museum in that skirt."

I sucked in a breath. His words were so raw, so sexual—it was a huge turn-on.

"Let me take you to my bedroom. I want you to lie down and get comfortable."

I nodded, letting him pull me to my feet, and left my shirt we'd discarded on the floor.

His room was handsomely decorated in black and white. Elegant and luxurious, but also strikingly simple, it fit him.

Arranging the pillows beneath my head, Cooper laid me out so I was comfortable on his massive king-sized bed.

With my skirt rucked up around my stomach, he hooked his fingers into the sides of my panties and drew them carefully down my legs and over my ankles. My bare flesh was already soaked, and as desperate as I was for his touch, I didn't know how to put into words what I wanted.

"Don't do that," he said softly.

"Do what?" I lifted up on my elbows to watch him move between my thighs.

"You're in your head, worrying about something you don't need to be. Just relax and let me make you feel good, okay?"

I smiled down at him. "Yes, Cooper."

He placed a soft kiss at the top of my pubic bone. "Good girl."

Rewarding me with a sweep of his tongue through my swollen lips, Cooper took his time, giving me playful licks and gentle nips.

"Promise me one thing."

His words surprised me. I opened my eyes and found his gaze on mine. "Yes?"

"You won't run off this time, will you?"

The sentiment behind his words hit me square in the chest. He didn't want me to feel the need to escape, like we'd done something wrong.

I appreciated that, so I nodded. Maybe we'd lie together and cuddle, or talk.

"Good. Then let me love this sweet little pussy."

Using his fingers to spread me apart, he nibbled gently on my clit with his teeth, and I felt his touch like a jolt of electricity. Moments later, his mouth covered me, his tongue swirling, circling—all his attention centered on that sensitive bundle of nerves, and *oh my God*. His mouth felt so incredibly warm against me, and he was extremely gifted at this.

Opening my eyes, I watched Cooper pleasure me. His eyes were closed, his expression soft. A smile tilted my lips when I noticed that as he lay on his stomach on the bed, his hips rutted uselessly against the mattress.

"Cooper," I murmured, so turned on by watching him.

"Yes, dove. Come for me."

Seconds later, my whole body went tight, my muscles tensing as wave after wave of delicious pleasure crashed through me.

When my senses returned, I gazed at Cooper, appreciating how truly beautiful he was. He'd shifted until we lay on our sides, facing each other, and I placed my hand on his jaw. He had such striking eyes, a sexy jaw, full lips, and that messy bedroom hair that I wanted to rake my fingers through. His size made me feel small, which wasn't easy—I never usually felt small or dainty. My curves had curves. But Cooper's broad muscled body and six-foot-four frame dwarfed mine. And I liked that.

But in this moment, it wasn't his looks I was noticing. It was how utterly giving this man was—bringing me pleasure and expecting nothing in return. That wasn't normal. And he was clearly turned on. His jeans had grown rather tight in the front.

"I'm so sorry. I swear, I'm not trying to be selfish."

He chewed on his lip—his erection was the elephant

in the room between us. "No pressure. You're doing fine."

He wasn't begging me to pet his one-eyed python, and for that, I was immensely grateful. Strangely, though? It only made me want to touch him more. He had such restraint, such control over his body, and apparently mine. The thought of making him feel even half as good as he'd made me feel was intoxicating.

He brushed my hair away from my face. "You've come so far. I'm just happy to see you enjoying yourself and not feeling any shame after."

I nodded. "You make me feel very good."

Those words were hard to say. They were so brutally honest, but it was the simple truth. Cooper wasn't concerned with his own release, or pushing me further than I was willing to go. He just gave—without expecting a damn thing in return. It made me want to reward him.

I swallowed the heavy lump in my throat as a tidal wave of bravery surged through me. I placed my hand on Cooper's denim-covered erection, and he sucked in a breath.

"Dove?"

I met his eyes. His green eyes had gone a shade darker with lust, and his voice was low and husky. He was so utterly sexy. So irresistible. I truly didn't know how I'd not done this sooner.

"I want to . . . try."

"Try?" he whispered, barely breathing.

I nodded, my confidence growing at the awareness of the effect I had on him. "I want to touch you."

Cooper's mouth curved into a lazy grin. "You can do any-fucking-thing you want to me."

I giggled. God, I loved how he did that. How he could immediately defuse any situation so I felt comfortable. I was coming to find I liked many things about him. The least of which were the orgasms he handed out like they were candy.

"I'm not experienced. I'm not . . ." I cleared my throat, pausing for a breath. *God, Corinne, pull it together.*

He quieted me with a soft kiss. "No judgment. No expectations."

Releasing the button of his jeans, I slowly lowered the zipper. Cooper lifted his hips so that when I tugged, his jeans and boxers slid easily down his hips.

Out sprang the most handsome cock I'd ever seen. Not that I had many to go by, but this thing was truly beautiful. Rigid and thick with a wide, rounded head, it was a work of art, belonging on something akin to Michelangelo's David—only the erotic version. There was hardly any hair covering him, he was neatly groomed, and I wasn't sure why that was something I noticed, but I guessed it was because I was taking in every detail like it might be my last time to see him like this, so exposed and vulnerable. So everything.

I lifted his cock from his belly, palming and playing with it like it was my new favorite toy.

"Christ," Cooper grunted.

I stared at him in wonder, honestly curious how he fit this thing in his pants. Because, seriously.

"You trying to kill me?" he murmured.

"Oh." I dropped his cock onto his belly where it gave a soft thwack. "I'm sorry. Did I hurt you?"

Amused, he petted my hair. "No."

Smiling with a new flash of bravery, I turned toward

him where we lay on our sides facing each other. Cooper brought his hands to my face, kissing me while I stroked his cock up and down until his breathing grew ragged, and I knew I was doing something right.

"That feel good?" I whispered.

"Jesus, dove." He moaned. "So good."

Spurred on by his soft need-filled noises, I continued working my hand up and down.

"A little faster, beautiful," he murmured.

I obeyed, my hand gliding over his thick shaft again and again. While we kissed deeply, his release shuddered through him, coating my hand in warm, sticky fluid.

Although I wouldn't know it until later, this moment would irrevocably change things between us forever.

Chapter Thirteen

Corinne

When I woke up the next morning surrounded by my own yellow and gray bed linens, I couldn't deny that I was a little bit disappointed. Being with Cooper, feeling him touch me ... it was like nothing I'd ever experienced before in my life, and the memory of his searing skin against mine was the sweetest of all.

And touching him, his thick manhood pumping semen between us? That made me feel hot all over again. God, I would have given almost anything to stay the night with him, to wake up in his strong arms and do it all over again. But, of course, I couldn't. I had responsibilities that he couldn't even imagine.

Rolling over in bed, I checked the time to make sure Aaron would still be asleep, then rolled to my feet and grabbed my phone before heading into the kitchen. It was Sunday, which meant he'd be expecting breakfast, and I was making scrambled eggs, his favorite.

Padding to the fridge, I opened the door and pulled out all the breakfast essentials before setting to work. But the more I clanked dishes against the counter, the more I found my mind drifting away from the task at hand and back to last night.

I sighed. Not for the first time, I wondered what Cooper was even doing with me. When I thought of him, I pictured him in his tailored business suit with his steely gray tie and that gorgeous face. He was the stuff of *GQ* magazine and Hollywood mixers. Successful, hardworking, affectionate, compassionate, and a million other things I wasn't.

And me? I was . . . curvy. That was a polite way to put it. Quiet, almost brooding sometimes. But on top of all of that, I was complicated. High-maintenance and complicated.

The last thing a guy like Cooper Kingsley needed was a girl who didn't fit in his world, a girl who could never be the kind of pinup stunner his brainy sister-in-law was . . . an easy charmer who looked like she had it all together.

I let out a deep breath through my nose as I whisked some eggs in a bowl and added an extra dose of cream for good measure.

Cooper and I didn't make sense together. The way he touched me, the way he made me feel? Both those things were beyond incredible, but they just didn't add up to a sum total that could possibly work out. And as we got closer, I needed to make sure I kept that at the forefront of my mind.

No lamenting over not staying in his bed. No fantasizing about the warm feel of his mouth against mine in the morning as we woke up side by side.

When we were together, I was going to cherish that time. But when we were apart? I had to remember who I was—and who he was. Where we stood. And if that wasn't enough, I needed to remember my mountain of responsibility for Aaron. That would do the trick.

If I could manage to do that, then this thing between us could be fun. Like a vacation to Jamaica before another long winter. Yes, that's what Cooper Kingsley was to me—a little break from my own stark reality.

The floorboards creaked, and I smiled to myself. Aaron was getting up and ready for his breakfast. I poured my mixture into the pan and checked the clock again before grabbing my phone from the table where I'd left it.

Scrolling through messages, I found a voice mail from Mauve and pressed the phone to my ear.

"Hey there, just checking in. Call me when you have the time, nothing earth-shattering."

The recording clicked off, and I frowned down at my cracked glass screen.

It had been too long since I'd gone for a visit. Between everything with Cooper and Aaron and the new job . . . There was no doubt Mauve would understand, but that didn't excuse me from the judgmental voice in my head, reminding me what a terrible friend I was.

The eggs on the range started to bubble and I stirred them around a little, sprinkling them with salt and pepper as I heard the floorboards creak more forcefully in the background. Sliding some eggs onto a plate, I left them at the table with a glass of orange juice for Aaron, and then slipped back into my own room to read the rest of my messages.

All ten of them were from Cooper.

> *12:00 A.M.: I already miss you.*

> *12:15 A.M.: Next time you should leave something here for me to remember you by. I'm thinking a pair of your panties might do the trick.*

My skin instantly prickled into goose bumps, and my

nipples went tight as I scrolled to the next message.

> *12:25 A.M.: Or better yet, bring all your panties here and just stop wearing them altogether.*
>
> *12:30 A.M.: I plan on checking to see if you follow through with this new plan when Monday comes around.*
>
> *1:00 A.M.: You've done something to me. I can't go a full two minutes without thinking about you.*

And on they went, including more imaginative details about what exactly he wanted to do when I came into work without my panties on Monday.

I blushed, smiling despite myself, and then the phone rang in my hand and I pressed it to my ear.

"Hello?" My voice was breathier than I would have liked, but then Mauve's husky voice filled my ear and I relaxed against my bed. Not feeling disappointed, exactly . . . just slightly deflated, was all.

"Well, if it isn't the busiest woman in Boston," Mauve teased.

"I know, I know. I've been a jerk," I muttered with a sigh.

She let out a raspy chuckle. "Don't be ridiculous. I'm

just nosy."

"Well, I'm here now. What's been going on?"

"Not a darn thing. Still beating off the men with sticks, you know. The nurses get them all jacked up on their medication, and suddenly they think they're Don Juan instead of an eighty-year-old retired dentist from Hoboken."

I laughed, affection closing around me like a warm hug. "I'm sure it's not all that bad."

"Oh, it is. That same dentist used a pickup line to let me know that he specializes in oral," she said with a cackle.

"Mauve!" I gasped on a laugh.

"Hey, I didn't say it. Though, to be honest, it's a hell of a selling point. I'll give him that."

"Oh my God," I muttered more to myself than into the phone. She was a riot, and I only hoped I had half as much good humor as she did if I lived to be her age.

"You don't want to hear about an old lady's dating life, though. Come on, tell me. What's kept you so busy? Or should I say who?"

I raised my eyebrows and sputtered, "Excuse me?"

"Oh, come on. I'm old; I'm not stupid. Suddenly you have more important things to do than sit around with an old lady or stay home and do nothing. So, what's his name, kiddo?"

I chewed on the inside of my cheek, weighing my options. Finally, I settled on, "Okay. Maybe there's kind of sort of someone. At work."

"I knew it. Hot damn. How's the sex?" she demanded.

"Mauve, oh my God," I murmured, my cheeks flaming. "No, no, we're just . . . taking it slow. And it's not serious. We just agreed to some light fun and nothing else."

"Where's the fun if there's no slap and tickle?" Mauve demanded.

"People can enjoy each other's company without having sex, you know."

"Maybe if those people aren't attracted to each other. Or if they don't count oral sex as actual sex. Is that the situation we've got here?"

"I refuse to answer that question," I shot back.

Mauve chuckled into the phone. "Okay, well, at least tell me why you're taking it slow and not serious?"

"I'm just . . ." I shook my head. "I'm not looking to date right now. It'd all be too complicated."

"Because this man at work has a small—"

I rushed to cut her off. "No! I'm not going there with you."

"So, what's the matter? Is he unattractive? Dull?" After a pause, she added, "Oh, jeez, does he make you listen to that terrible rap music?"

"He doesn't do any of that. He's perfect. It's me. I'm just . . . it's just not what I'm looking for."

"Because of Aaron."

It wasn't a question, so I didn't bother to answer it.

A beat of silence stretched between us, and then Mauve cleared her throat. "You know, I think this talk is long overdue."

"What talk?"

"This one. The one where I remind you what you

already know in your heart. Aaron would want you to be happy. You did a good thing by him, but you can't allow that to rule the rest of your life, especially not with as young as you are. When you're a little old lady like me, you'll want memories of this time to look back on fondly."

"I know, it's just—"

"You don't know, though," Mauve said, not unkindly. "You can't know. But I don't want you to live your whole life and then look back and realize there's nothing to see in the rearview mirror. Do you understand?"

I swallowed. "I think so."

"Good. Now, I know it's Sunday and you're probably cooking, so I won't keep you. I just missed the sound of your voice."

"Thanks. I'll see you soon."

We said our good-byes, and I hung up the phone before tossing it into my sea of covers. I didn't want to look at it for a while. In fact, for now, all I wanted to do was lie back and think about Cooper. And me. And everything Mauve had said.

But as soon as I closed my eyes, there was a knock on my bedroom door. Aaron was waiting for me, ready to share in our morning tradition.

"Coming," I called.

But my heart was somewhere across town, in bed with a man I could never hope to keep.

Chapter Fourteen

Cooper

I sighed, glancing at my digital calendar as I tried for the fourteenth time that morning to rearrange my meetings in some way that allowed me to squeeze the most into my day. Too bad that wasn't the only thing on my mind. As I shifted one mixer and another golf outing, I stared at the orange highlighted dates on the screen. They were colored but blank—I hadn't typed the words on the calendar, but I knew what they meant.

Time with Corinne.

In the past three weeks since our night at the museum, we'd seen each other three or four times a week, but try as I might, there was still something between us. An invisible wedge. A bridge that I wasn't allowed to cross.

Not that I hadn't tried. I'd taken her to movies and readings and art galleries. Cooked her dinner at my place and asked her every question I could think of—her favorite television show, her favorite toy as a kid, her childhood best friend's name. She answered me patiently, but in spite of all my efforts, I felt like I still didn't know her. The real her. Like there was something she was keeping from me.

But it was more than that. As the weeks wore on, I started to notice little quirks. Like how we could never head back to her apartment after a night out. She never stayed over at my place, either. And when I'd suggested going away for a weekend? She'd flatly refused, saying "it simply wasn't possible."

I'd tried to be patient, but it was getting to the point that I couldn't be patient much longer. Not without some explanation beyond the one she always gave. That her life was just too complicated for anything more than what we were doing. That she appreciated the sex and the company, but we could never be anything more.

And for now? I was taking what I could get.

Not because I didn't want more—I wanted everything. But if she wasn't willing to give herself to me completely? Well, I wasn't willing to let go of what little parts of her I could have.

She was incredible. Smart and driven at work, punctual and professional. And in bed? She was better than anyone I'd ever been with. So needy and responsive.

So thirsty for more.

Even if I'd wanted to, I couldn't walk away from her. Not now. Not yet.

But that didn't stop me from daydreaming about what else we could be. About what she might be like when that wall of ice around her heart melted away and she finally let me in.

Tapping my calendar for the millionth time, I added another orange dot to the night of the company mixer—a hopeful dot—and then buzzed Corinne to head into my office.

Within five minutes, she appeared, her red pencil skirt clinging to her hips and showing off her perfect hourglass frame. Her hair was pulled into a professional knot at the nape of her neck, and I imagined running my fingers through her silky locks until they tumbled all around her face.

"Good morning," I said, careful to remind myself of the professional atmosphere we'd sworn to maintain.

"Morning," she said, her cheeks slightly pink as she smiled at me.

My body responded instantly, but I forced myself to focus.

"I have a list of things we need to go over before the gala this weekend. Will you take a seat?" I motioned to the leather chair across from my desk and she slipped into it easily, setting her clipboard on her knee as she waited for me to speak.

I cleared my throat, trying my best not to stare at the faintest hint of cleavage that peeked out from her button-down top, and then glanced at the list of questions in front of me, delegating each task while ensuring she had everything else in order.

As always, she was rock steady and had everything under admirable control.

"Anything else?" she asked when my battery of questions had finally been satisfied.

I glanced at the closed door, letting my imagination run away with me for a moment. I could ask for so, so much more, but instead I said, "Just having some trouble with my calendar. Too many events, not enough hours in the day."

"Want me to take a look?" she asked. "See if I can

reschedule some things or take them off your plate?"

"Sure."

I motioned to the computer screen in front of me and she rounded my desk, leaning over to study my schedule and putting her ass on full, perfect display. She shifted slightly, her pouty mouth pursed as she tried to make sense of all I had to do. But then, when she jutted her hip out to the side, it was too much.

I wrapped my hands around her waist and pulled her into my lap side-saddle, kissing the creamy length of her neck until I reached the shell of her ear.

"You tricked me," she murmured breathlessly.

"I didn't mean to. You're just so damn hot," I murmured, nibbling on her earlobe.

"Cooper . . . someone could come in."

"So what? I'm the boss," I whispered, blowing lightly into her ear. "And no one but you comes in without knocking. Don't make me stop."

"I have to." She squirmed a little but stayed in my lap all the same. "We agreed not to mix work and pleasure."

"Okay, I'll stop, but only if you reconsider coming

away with me next weekend," I said, pulling back and fighting the ache in my swollen cock.

She shook her head. "I told you. I can't."

"Not ever? Do you turn into a pumpkin at midnight or something? Were you cursed by an evil witch?"

She rolled her eyes. "Of course not, silly. I just can't. It's complicated."

"I'm starting to learn that a lot about you is complicated," I said softly as I released her, both sexually and emotionally frustrated.

She cupped my jaw and held my gaze with her solemn one. "It's the truth."

"All I want is to get to know you. I feel like there are parts of you, even after all this time together, that I just don't know or understand."

"And that bothers you?" she asked.

"It bothers me when I feel like there's something between us, yeah. I know part of the reason you agreed to this arrangement was so that you could feel more comfortable in the bedroom. Tell me, do you?"

"I do," she said, her voice low as her lean throat

worked.

"So, what's going on? We enjoy each other's company. We're magic in the sack. What's holding you back?" I asked, unable to hold it in any longer.

She considered me for a long moment and then let out a shuddery breath, locking her gaze somewhere over my shoulder. "Do you want to know why I never felt comfortable in bed? I mean, other than my general lack of experience?"

I managed to nod, but an ominous feeling slid through me suddenly, and I took her hand. "You don't have to—"

She shook her head and pressed on. "It's not a story I like to talk about, but when I was thirteen . . ." She took a shaky breath and started again, the words coming out in a rush. "When I was thirteen, I lived in a foster home with relatively few kids. That was a first for me. The parents were older, and they had a nineteen-year-old son who was home for the summer from college. Everyone was nice to me, but the son . . . he was too nice."

I stayed silent, not wanting to interrupt or derail the rare moment of vulnerability, but nausea slicked my belly.

"One night, late, he sneaked into my room, and he, um, he touched me. Inappropriately. He said it would be our little secret and told me not to tell."

I gritted my teeth, fighting the urge to howl with outrage. To somehow find the bastard, even now, and rip out his beating heart.

"I didn't say anything, at first." Corinne swallowed hard. "But then I finally told. His parents didn't believe me, or if they did, they did nothing about it and expected me to just grin and bear it. I managed to avoid him until my caseworker came to the house for a check, and I immediately told her what happened. She took me from the home that very day. Ever since then, sexual contact has been . . . difficult for me." She stared at the far corner of the room, refusing to meet my gaze.

"I'm so sorry. Did he—" I stopped myself, not wanting to press. Still, I had to know. Had her first time been that? Rape? The story was sickening enough, but that would make it even worse. God, how could she even let me touch her after that kind of violation?

She shook her head. "It could have been much worse than it was. He didn't rape me. My first time was when I was much older."

My hands remained fisted at my sides.

"Thanks for telling me all that. I know it was hard for you, and it explains a lot. You're such a warrior," I said, shaking my head, even more in awe of her.

She gave me a shaky smile. "I just did what I had to do. And it was about time I told you. It's not a story I tell much, is all."

"I can understand that. It's a big thing to trust someone with. So, thank you for giving me that trust."

A moment of silence passed between us as she leaned back against me, and I wrapped my arms around her waist. She sighed and I breathed deep, drinking in the scent of her perfume as my mind drifted again.

Even after all of that, though, everything she shared, I knew that there was more. A whole room of ghosts still locked away. I could feel it in the tension of her body, see it in the worried lines on her face. And as furious and sick and terrible as her admission had made me feel, if there was more, I wanted to know it. I wanted to make it all better, in some small way.

"So," I said, breaking the silence, "I've been thinking."

"You don't say," she teased.

Ignoring her, I pressed on. "I've been thinking, and I was wondering if, with all this extra help in the bedroom and your newfound sexual confidence, you might be able to date soon."

"*Date* date?" She raised her eyebrows and I nodded.

"I don't think so." The teasing light disappeared from her eyes, and those worry lines returned with a vengeance.

"Why not?"

She chewed on her bottom lip, then shook her head. "You know, I've been thinking a lot about this too. For the past few weeks, actually. Cooper, you're a great guy—"

"Don't," I shot back, stiffening. "Don't do that. You're not ending our arrangement. We're too damned good together."

It took everything I had not to remind her of that here and now.

"No," she said carefully. "I'm not. But just because I'm not ready to date doesn't mean you shouldn't. I don't want to hold you back. I mean, you're a really great guy, and I have no doubt you're going to find someone amazing. When you do, I'll just fade into the background with lots of fond memories. The point is, if someone catches your eye? Go for it. Ask her on a date. Just because we agreed not to sleep with other people doesn't mean you can't keep your options open."

"I still don't understand why I can't date *you*," I said. "We do everything else together."

She pursed her lips. "Look, this job, the sex, you—it's all more than I could have hoped for in my wildest dreams, but I'm not ready for a committed relationship like that, and I know that you are. Don't mistake this for something it's not, Cooper. I'm not available the way you want me to be."

Her words dug into my heart like sharp talons, but I nodded all the same, pretending I didn't feel the ache of her rejection. At least she wasn't ending our arrangement. That was the best I could hope for now, and it was something.

"Fine, we're not dating, but I do need someone to accompany me to the gala this weekend," I said.

"Cooper—"

"Just hear me out. We don't have to make it a date. We can go as friends, but I don't have time to get out there and find someone, and I certainly don't want to go by myself."

"Why not?"

"Because it's work related, and it makes me look bad to not have a date. I'm going as a glorified babysitter. The mixer is just for the girls and our clients to meet, so the clients have better context when they browse the online database, and I'll only be there to make sure nobody gets too drunk and humps in the bathroom. Believe me, I highly doubt there will be time for romance. Think of it as more of a work function."

She laughed. "Sounds like a fun night. A work function where our job is to keep people from humping in the bathrooms. How could I say no to that?"

"Exactly. So don't. Date or not, just come with me."

She frowned, surveying me with those dreamy blue eyes of hers. Finally, she said, "Okay, I'll go. But I'm telling you, the food better be incredible if I'm going to have to break up drunk people grinding on each other."

"Only the best for you." I grinned. "Promise."

In spite of my smile, there was a chill settling in my bones. She'd told me the darkest of secrets, something that had shaped her entire life from childhood, and I knew in my gut we'd only scratched the surface.

I stared at her beautiful face as she stood, and swallowed the question hammering against my lips.

What are you hiding, Corinne?

Chapter Fifteen

Corinne

By the time three o'clock rolled around on Saturday afternoon, I'd already tried on—and discarded—roughly eight dresses, seven skirts, and one ill-conceived romper that made me look like a plump toddler, only with big boobs.

Panic was setting in when there was a knock on the door. I answered it, my button-down shirt only half tucked into my poodle pajama bottoms while curlers pulled at my roots and made my eyes water.

"Hello?" I said without thinking, only to find the postal worker standing at my door, her nose wrinkled as she looked up at me.

"Package," she said.

"Who for?" I asked. "I didn't order anything."

"Listen, lady, I just drop stuff off." She thrust four boxes toward me, and I took them all before she unceremoniously bustled away.

Closing the door, I glanced down to find that all the boxes were addressed to me, and I carried them into my bedroom with no small amount of anticipation.

Quickly, I peeled away the tape on the first box and found a steely blue-gray pearl necklace inside with a matching bracelet and earrings.

"Beautiful," I murmured to myself as I slid on the bracelet, tossing aside the box to open the next. This one contained matching strappy heels. Next came a box with only a black bustier inside, but no matching panties. The last box contained a dress.

But it wasn't just a dress, not really. It was *the* dress. I winced, one eye closed, before I glanced at the size, only to find that it was exactly right.

The dress was black and gun-metal gray, perfect to set off my new pearls and shoes, and I hugged it close to me as a rush of emotion washed over me. It was like Cooper had sensed my panic from all the way across the city and had come to my rescue. Again.

If only things could have been different . . . another time, another place.

Nope. Not going there. I had a free pass tonight. A guilt-free "not really a date" with Cooper, and I wasn't about to ruin it with self-pity.

And judging by the expression on the mail lady's face, I had a whole lot of work to do before I put that dress on.

Rushing around the apartment, I gave Aaron his medication and fed him an early dinner before shaving my legs and putting on some hasty makeup. My heated curlers were finally beginning to cool, and when I pulled them from my hair, I heard the chime of the doorbell again.

Frantic, I glanced at the clock. It was already almost five thirty. It must be Cooper, and though he was early, it wasn't by much.

"Shoot," I muttered, pulling on my thigh-high stockings before running into the hall and sliding as I tried to stop.

"Aaron, will you go in your room for a little while?" I asked, though I didn't wait for a response as I wheeled him down the hall at top speed wearing nothing but my bustier, slip, and stockings. Half my head was still in curlers, and I winced as the doorbell rang again and I snapped Aaron's door closed.

What was Cooper thinking? I'd never let him inside before. I'd never even let him get as far as the front door.

But the doorbell chimed again, and seeing no other option, I ran to the front of the apartment and flung the door open.

"Hey," I said, practically panting. "I'm running a little behind."

Cooper grinned, his gaze trailing over me, leaving a path of heat in its wake. "I can see that. Mind if I come in?"

Yes.

"No, of course not. I'll just, um, be a minute." I unrolled curlers as I spoke, and when he nodded, I rushed to my bedroom and yanked the dress over my head, ripping curlers from my hair at a pace that made my eyes well up with tears.

"Fight through the pain," I told myself, gritting my teeth as I brushed the curls into waves and double-checked my makeup before spraying on perfume. Finally, I slipped on the rest of the jewelry and my heels and clicked toward the door, flinging it open to find Aaron on the other side, smack dab in the middle of the hallway.

My eyes widened and I glanced from him to Cooper, who still looked unconcerned as he waited near the front door.

Anticipating his question, I said to Aaron, "Leftovers in the fridge. I'm going out, but I'll be back later."

He nodded and then rolled down the hall to the kitchen, not bothering to look twice at Cooper.

I took a deep breath, turning on my heel and preparing to see the inevitable pity or confusion in Cooper's eyes. I didn't want to face that, didn't want to answer his questions and explain everything that had happened to make Aaron the way he was.

Didn't want to have to tell him what Aaron meant to me.

But looking at Cooper, I wasn't sure I would have to. There was interest in his eyes, to be sure, but also grim acceptance.

He simply looked at me and said, "You look incredible. Are you ready to go?"

Swallowing hard, I nodded and allowed him to lead me out and toward the car. When I was safely stowed in the passenger's seat, I stared out at the evening sky.

"Looks like it's going to rain," I said, desperate to

find something, anything that I could focus on other than Cooper's inevitable curiosity.

"It does. I should have sent you a coat too."

I turned and offered him a trembling smile, the fear of what was to come on hold at the reminder of his sweet gesture. "You did more than enough. Thank you, by the way. You saved my life."

"I'm not sure it was all that heroic." Cooper grinned. "But if you're willing to give me that much credit, I'll take it."

He started the car and drove onto the street as I watched him from the corner of my eye. The question was on the tip of his tongue. It had to be. It was such a normal, everyday sort of thing to ask.

But he didn't ask it. He didn't ask anything at all. He only drove, the soft sounds of indie music playing on the radio as we went.

For a moment, I considered bringing it up, clearing the air to save myself from the inevitable questions he would ask. But I wasn't ready, not yet. And I think Cooper knew it too.

• • •

A few short minutes later, Cooper handed off his keys to a valet in front of a swanky downtown hotel. The foyer was crammed with beautiful women in dresses that were almost as stunning as my own, and middle-aged business types who couldn't stop staring at them.

When Cooper walked in, he charmed everyone in turn, greeting most of them by name as we sailed through the crowd and made our way toward a gorgeous ballroom complete with marble floors and high, molded ceilings.

"This place is incredible," I said, feeling a little breathless.

"We like to do things right. Have I mentioned how exquisite you look tonight, by the way?"

"You might have."

"Allow me to remind you." He tucked a strand of my hair behind my ear, then kissed my cheek before guiding me to the nearest group of men and women, then the next and the next.

I met hedge fund managers and lawyers, doctors and venture capitalists. Women who had their degrees in biochemical engineering and physics.

With each of them, Cooper was just as charismatic and genuine as he'd been with the last. When someone was coarse, he was there to be their buffer. If someone was timid, he coaxed them out of their shell. He made them all laugh and open up, smoothing those awkward moments in everyday social interactions that might have gone on forever if it wasn't for his easy wit.

And I was by his side for all of it, his firm hand warm and reassuring in mine as we moved from one group to the next.

This, I supposed, was what my life could have been like if things had worked out differently. In another world, I could have had a man like this—strong and confident and charming. Someone who might hold me at night when I had a bad dream, or soothe my worries when they threatened to overwhelm me. Someone to share the burden and ease the tension.

Someone to love me. To care for me and take care of me.

A waitress passed by and I grabbed a glass of champagne, taking a steadying sip as Cooper launched into a funny anecdote, though I could barely hear him. I was too focused on my own thoughts, my own selfish regrets.

Like it or not, this wasn't the course my life had taken. Long ago, I'd made my peace with that. Dredging up all that heartache and desperation now would do neither of us any good. My life was my life . . . it was as simple as that.

One day Cooper would have the full package, a woman who would be there for him emotionally in ways I simply couldn't. He deserved that much, and I had to let him have it.

But maybe not tonight.

For tonight, in this moment, we were together, and I didn't want to waste another moment of that. The future would come at us hard and fast, ripping away what little we did have. Before that time came, I was going to grab this precious opportunity and squeeze every drop of pleasure from it that I could.

Cooper laughed as we disconnected from another group and walked toward the bar. I sat my barely touched drink on the counter and smiled at him, my mind spinning with possibilities.

"I think things are going well," he said. "Doesn't look like anyone is looking to hump in the bathroom just yet."

My grin widened. "Maybe not them, but I have a few ideas."

His crooked smile was lazy and confident all at once, but his eyes went instantly hot. "What are you thinking, you little devil?"

I slid one finger along his silk tie. "I think you know exactly what I'm thinking. Now, come on, does this place have a coat closet or something?"

"What's gotten into you?" Cooper asked, his voice raspy as he leaned in closer.

"Are you saying you don't want to go?" I raised an eyebrow and he took my hand.

"Forget I said anything," he growled, leading me to a hallway in the far corner of the room and slipping into a coat closet halfway down. I giggled as he closed the door behind us.

Silently, we hid behind the longest of the coats. In the darkness, Cooper kissed me firm and sweet, pressing his hard body against me, but I wasn't interested in that.

Not now.

Suddenly desperate to make him feel like the whole world, as cherished as he made me feel, I dropped to my knees in front of him, fumbling quickly with his buckle before ripping down his pants and boxers in one tug.

"Corinne . . ."

Before he could say another word, I grasped his shaft, working him up and down with steady, sure strokes. Already firm, he grew as hard as steel.

"Let me do this, Cooper. I need to taste you, to touch you."

He leaned back against the paneled walls, closing his eyes, and I took him into my mouth, sucking gently as I rolled my tongue over his swollen head.

"Damn," he groaned. "That's so fucking hot."

I hummed my approval, then took him deeper into my mouth, so deep that he hit the back of my throat as I did, but I didn't care. I simply gripped the rest of him, stroking what I couldn't fit into my mouth as I worked him up and down, loving the way his fingers weaved in my hair and urged me to move faster, to love him harder.

In this moment, I was with him, and I wanted him to know what it was to be with me—needed to show him how much I cared for him and wanted him. Needed him to feel all the things I could never say aloud.

He groaned louder, his hips flexing against me now. "Yes, baby, just like that."

I pulled him deeper, pushing myself to the limit as I sucked and stroked him. The last of his control seemed to slip away as he thrust frantically into my mouth, his fingers tightening in my hair. I moaned around him, letting the vibration ripple over his thick, hard cock.

"I'm going to come," he managed through gritted teeth, and I gripped him harder still, sucking firmly until he finally lost himself with a cry.

I held fast as he came, spurting into my mouth in hot, greedy pulses. We stayed that way for long moments, me savoring his salty taste and the sounds of his harsh breaths, him stroking my hair almost lovingly.

It was sensual and sweet, and tears pricked the back of my eyelids.

I pulled away, wiping my mouth on the back of my hand, relishing the sweet heat of my now-swollen lips. I rose unsteadily to my feet, more moved than I should have been, but I managed a shaky smile.

"So, boss man, how do we go back to the party without everyone knowing what we did?"

"We don't," he muttered, yanking me close for a hard kiss before releasing me. "You're coming home with me right now. I'm not going to wait any longer to have you."

Chapter Sixteen

Cooper

I wasn't sure if Corinne expected a slow lesson in seduction—the controlled and methodic removal of each piece of clothing before finally making our way to the bed.

But this wasn't that.

Once we were tucked inside my penthouse, I kicked the door shut, pulling her to my chest as my mouth crashed down onto hers. The way she'd pleasured me in the coat closet wasn't nearly enough to satiate my want for her.

In a heartbeat, we were kissing deeply, grasping, clawing at each other as we fought to get even closer.

"Tell me to stop. Tell me to be careful with you."

"No." Her eyes met mine with a clash of want and need. "Take me how you need me."

After weeks of careful foreplay, now that this moment was here, I couldn't seem to make myself stop and go slow with her. Lifting her into my arms, I marched us back toward my bedroom in easy strides. Soon, she was stripped completely bare, and though I wanted to stand there like some love-struck prick and admire her, Corinne was just as wild, grasping at my belt and all but ripping open my pants.

I was all too happy to oblige her.

"We have all night," I reminded her, dropping a kiss to her collarbone.

She shook her head. "Need you. Please, Coop." Her voice was a soft plea, and here in the darkness of my bedroom, I knew it would be impossible to slow down. We'd been building to this moment for too long.

After wrestling my unruly dick into a condom, I joined her on the bed, moving between her thighs. "Tell me if I do something you don't like . . ."

Corinne shook her head. "I want you."

Kissing her deeply, I sensed she was ready. And when she lifted her hips, rubbing her wet pussy along the underside of my shaft, I knew she was right. The time for conversation was over.

Lining myself up between her thighs, I began to push in slowly.

She was so tight, so amazingly perfect. It took her

body a moment to adjust and accommodate mine, and while that happened, she whimpered and shifted restlessly beneath me. I couldn't take my eyes off her. All that flushed pink skin and those ample curves. She was so hot and responsive beneath me.

"I'm sorry," she whimpered.

"Don't," I warned. I drew a breath in slowly as I eased myself inside. "It's been a while, yeah?"

She nodded, and though I wanted to hear her story, wanted to know why she kept herself locked away in some ivory tower like a princess, I didn't press. I couldn't have formed the thoughts coherently right now even if I'd wanted to.

"I'll go slow. Tell me that you're okay, dove."

Her gaze latched onto mine as she clung to my biceps.

God, she made me feel so big, so fucking powerful, that I was lost. Lost to everything about this woman—her scent, the sweet pleasure-filled sounds she was making, the grip of her body around mine. It was so, so good. I didn't think anything, ever, had felt better. Not to mention how hard she'd made me work to get here. We'd been out countless times. I'd wooed her and lusted after her, craving her until I practically couldn't take it anymore. I'd have given her anything she asked for in that moment.

"You're so big. But I love it."

I placed one hand beneath her head, cradling her there, the other planted flat against the bed as I began moving my hips in slow, deliberate thrusts. She made me feel out of control and grounded all at once.

"Talk to me, beautiful," I groaned out through a rush of breath. "How does it feel?"

"So good. So, so good," she whispered, her breaths coming fast now.

"Is this how you like it?"

She nodded, and I felt the movement of her head bob where it was tucked against my throat. "You're perfect."

I knew exactly what she meant.

Everything about this moment was exquisitely, painfully perfect. Like it would never again be this shiny, this new, this amazing ever again.

But the sweet, blissful friction building between us

refused to be ignored. As Corinne became more vocal, more eager—tilting her pelvis to meet mine, thrusting against me in time with my strokes—I began to move a little faster.

We'd never had intercourse, so as much as I wanted to think I knew her body by now, I didn't want to take anything for granted. Now wasn't the time to get cocky. This was about wringing as much pleasure from her body as I could.

"Dove," I groaned, sliding back until we were still connected, but just barely.

She let out a frustrated sound at the loss of me. God, that sound was addicting.

"Just need to know if you'll come like this, or if you need more," I whispered.

"More, please," she said on a sigh.

I could have chuckled. She'd transformed so much from the shy girl I'd embarrassed in my office. Now she was a confident, mature woman, willing to vocalize what she needed in bed. It had been a beautiful transformation.

"Yes, ma'am."

I groaned, sliding back inside her. Angling my hips with each thrust to press against her inner walls, I slid my fingers between us, rubbing her clit in gentle circles. She made a wordless sound of pleasure, and a smile blossomed on my lips.

"You are so sexy." Leaning down to kiss her lips, I whispered all the beautiful things she meant to me while she writhed beneath me.

My thrusts strengthened, my hips pinning her to the mattress as my own climax grew near. After a few minutes more, I knew I couldn't hold off much longer. She felt so incredibly good—so fucking tight—and she was so responsive, my orgasm was like a freight train bearing down on me.

"Come for me, dove," I whispered.

Corinne was so close, and my words seemed to shove her over the edge. "Yes, Cooper. Yes, yes." She moaned, nipping and sucking against my throat as she trembled beneath me.

The moment her pussy tightened around me, my own climax ripped through me. My cock bucked almost violently inside her as the most powerful orgasm I'd ever had shattered through me.

"Fuck." Rolling to my side, I mourned the loss of her body. I wasn't generally a cuddler—at least, I hadn't been in a long time—but tugging her against my chest was a powerful instinct. I needed her close, needed her safe. I needed her to understand that I would protect her, that I would look out for her needs. Emotional, physical, all of them.

Still out of breath, I gasped out, "That was . . ."

"Everything," she finished for me.

Chapter Seventeen

Corinne

"You sure you don't want to come along?" Alyssa asked, rising to her feet and grabbing her purse. "I swear if I don't get out of this place for at least an hour every day, my head will literally explode. Nobody wants that."

I smiled at her and shook my head. "No, I swear. I'm fine. I have some stuff I need to handle."

"Stuff like slipping into Cooper's office and—"

"*Stuff* stuff," I cut in, my cheeks heating. "Like none-of-your-business stuff."

Alyssa sniffed and lifted her chin. "Fine, then."

I rolled my eyes. "You're not insulted. You are like the hardest person in the universe to insult. You're like titanium."

She placed a hand on her hip and quirked her mouth to the side. "I'm not insulted. It's just not like you to get all sassy with me. I'm nosy, so I was hoping that if I played all wounded, you'd feel bad and offer me some crumb of juicy gossip. But, apparently, you've toughened up. Can't blame a girl for trying." She yanked her trendy purse onto her shoulder and grinned at me. "Want me to bring you anything back?"

"A warm chocolate-chip cookie if the cart is there today." I fumbled for my purse to get her some money, but she shrugged me off.

"I've got it this time. You owe me a cookie run in the future."

"Deal."

She scuttled away and disappeared behind the elevator doors with a ding before I settled back into my emails.

I would have loved to say that all of these were strictly professional, that I was so devoted to my job that I couldn't leave for my lunch break that day. But the truth was that I was majorly behind on a project I'd been working on for months, and as of Monday, everything had been falling apart.

A charity festival for the orphanage in the heart of the city was scheduled for tomorrow, and though I'd spent weeks meticulously organizing the pie contest, dunking booth, and story hour, it seemed like everything was unraveling faster than a poorly knit sweater in a washing machine.

The storyteller's baby was sick, the dunk tank was double-booked, and the pie-contest judges had suddenly decided to go on gluten-free diets. And that wasn't even to mention the politics of trying to figure out which volunteer wouldn't work with another volunteer because she may or may not have slept with the first volunteer's husband. The politics of this was unlike anything I'd ever seen before.

In short, it was a nightmare, but with only twenty-four hours to fix it, I was determined to make my lunch hour count. So I started with the story-time lady, a woman from a neighboring suburb who was apparently the Meryl Streep of book narration. I dialed her, waited as the phone rang twice, then took a deep breath as someone picked up on the other end. In the background, a baby was screaming while a man's voice seemed to be shouting back.

"Hello?" a tired-sounding woman murmured.

"Janine? Hi, this is Corinne from the Hearts for Saint Joseph's Carnival—"

"Oh, hi," Janine said in a rush. "Look, I know why

you're calling, but I really can't come. I haven't slept in three days, and any idiot can read an Amelia Bedelia book. I'm sorry, but you have to find someone else."

"I understand, but if you could just consider the children. They—"

The line went dead, letting me know that Janine was definitely out, and I sighed before setting down the receiver.

"Everything okay?" a familiar deep voice asked, and I looked up to find Cooper a few paces from my desk, his brows knit in concern.

I shook my head. "Yes. I mean, no. Like, yes. Nobody is dying . . ."

"But everything isn't okay?"

I rested my face in my hands and then peeked up at him through my fingers. "Everything with the company is fine. All the dates are set up, and no cancellations so far today."

"I wasn't asking about the company. I was asking about you. What's going on?"

I swallowed and forced myself to meet his gaze. "It's

sort of a lot to explain. See, ever since I . . . graduated out of the system, I've volunteered for the orphanage to try and make sure the kids have toys and books and anything else they might need so that they can be kids, you know?"

"Noble of you." Cooper nodded, his warm gaze already calming me some.

"But that's not really the point. The point is that I've spent the better part of this year planning the big fall carnival for the orphanage, and everything is falling apart."

"What's everything?" he asked.

"Well, we're having a pie contest and the judges backed out."

"So, select a lucky ten people to taste and have them vote by ballot." He shrugged.

I blinked. "Right. Of course. That's an easy answer. I don't know why I didn't think of that."

"Because you're too worked up."

"Maybe." I sighed. "But it's more than that. The dunk tank got double-booked, and the story-time lady canceled too."

"I know a dunk-tank guy. And, as a matter of fact, I can tell one hell of a story."

I blinked. "How on earth do you know a dunk-tank guy?"

"I also know a glassblower, a hit man, a sword swallower, and a guy who makes tables out of recycled cans. You'd be amazed at the kind of connections you can make in this job."

I smiled at him, relief rushing through me along with another warmer feeling I refused to name. "I just need the dunk-tank guy, but I'll take the hit man's name in case anyone else dares to cancel on me," I joked, blinking back relieved tears.

"Sure thing. I'll give him a call, but I doubt it's going to be a problem. In fact, our company will donate the dunk tank."

I shook my head, quickly doing the math and realizing I could use those extra funds as a head start on the Christmas jubilee. "Wow, Cooper. I don't know how to thank you. You . . ."

"Saved the day? Yeah, I know." He cracked his knuckles. "Now, what book am I reading?"

I shook my head again, a little more forcefully this time. "No, you don't have to do that. I can find someone or do it myself or—"

"You're going to be busy running this whole thing. Let me help you. I insist. Should I pick the book myself, or . . ."

I raised my eyebrows. "The kids voted on *Delilah and the Dragon Slayer*. I have a copy of it."

"I can do that." He grinned. "What time do you want me to pick you up? I'm guessing you'll need help setting up too?"

"Uh, the carnival starts at noon."

"So I'm guessing we need to get to the park or wherever by eight?"

I stared up at him blankly, though I knew better than to argue. "Yeah, eight works."

• • •

Standing in the church parking lot while Cooper directed the pie contestants and dunk-tank operators, I blinked back a wave of emotion.

When would I learn? When would I get it through

my thick skull that Cooper Kingsley was the kind of man who was desperate to fix any problems that sprang up around him?

From the second he showed up at my apartment this morning, he made a list of things we had to do, and immediately rolled up his sleeves when we got here.

I'd barely had to lift a finger all morning, and now that guests were finally starting to filter in, I could see the joy on his face as he greeted families and kids.

If I was smart, I might have sent him home right there and then. Thanked him for his time and sent him packing. After all, our agreement was for strings-free sex, not afternoons of charity work and laughter. Still, I couldn't bring myself to turn him away. Couldn't bear to see him leave. But every second longer I spent at his side, I was falling harder. Deeper.

And pretty soon, I'd be in big, big trouble.

Careful to make sure he didn't notice, I watched him as he made his way toward me, that damned white smile of his still stretched across his handsome face.

"So, what's the verdict, boss? We free to enjoy ourselves now?" he asked when he was finally in earshot of me.

I looked up, pretending it was the first time I'd noticed him, and offered my own smile in return.

"You did a fine job today," I said. "The kids are going to have a great time."

"I think they will, yeah." Cooper nodded. "But what about you? Are you going to take some time to enjoy yourself?"

I shrugged. "I don't know. You know the old saying . . . a carnival commissioner's job is never done."

"Says who? Come on, you're not even going to check out story time? We're starting in a little while. I know you're a big *Delilah and the Dragon Slayer* fan," he teased.

"Who told you my secret?" I laughed.

"Come on. Stay through story time and I might even get you a hot dog afterward."

I frowned, but damn it, I didn't want to say no. I nodded as he led me into the little semicircle filled with carpet samples and one folding chair for the storyteller.

A few kids and their parents were already hovering around, chatting with each other while the space filled up.

But in a matter of fifteen minutes, there was little room to stand, let alone sit.

Cooper took his place, smiling at everyone who'd gathered there, and when it was finally time to start, he clapped his hands together and brought everyone's attention to him.

"Hey, everyone! We're going to start today with a little game. Now, when I say *one*, I want you to say *two*, okay? Ready? One!"

The kids yelled back, "Two!"

Cooper said, "Nice job. Thanks, guys."

I'd wondered what he was doing, but I smiled when I realized he just needed the rowdy crowd to quiet down. His little trick had managed it so quickly, so easily, just like he did everything.

Cooper took a seat in the chair, continuing. "We're going to read a really awesome book today, but I'm going to need a friend to help me get this right. I'm not sure she's ready, so you'll need to cheer her on with me, okay?"

I blushed, sensing the coming storm, but there was nothing I could do. In a matter of seconds, Cooper had started the crowd in chanting my name, and I walked toward his throne, my whole body radiating heat.

"What are you doing?" I asked from the corner of my mouth, but he only beamed up at me.

"Now, Corinne is shy, but we have to help her be brave like Delilah. Would you guys like if Corinne played Delilah today?"

From behind the chair, he pulled out a pink cone-shaped hat entirely covered in glitter with a long pink scarf dangling from the top. He stood, fixing it to my head before placing a plastic golden crown on his own head.

"I came prepared," he said with a wink.

"Now, Corinne—or should I say, Princess Delilah—and I are going to act out the book for you guys. Would you like that?" he asked, and the kids all cheered.

Without another word, Cooper reached for the book and launched into the story, sharing the pages with me so I could read the dialogue and act out my part in the dragon-slaying tale.

It was silly, I knew, but part of me felt more alive in that moment than I had in a long time. I gripped Cooper's chest as the dragon came closer to us, and then saved him when it lurched, slaying the mighty beast with a dollar-store foam sword that had become magical to both me and the kids watching.

They held their breath as Cooper got to his feet, clutching the place where the dragon had wounded him.

"Princess," he choked out. "I'm dying."

The front row gasped.

"No," I cried, pressing the back of my hand to my forehead. "You can't leave me! You can't!"

"There is only one solution. True love's kiss." He let out a pathetic cough.

I pulled his face to mine, kissing him swiftly before losing myself and deepening the kiss slightly—at least, until I heard the chorus of *aw*s and *ew*s from the children all around us.

When I pulled away, Cooper sprang to his feet, his life restored. "Princess Delilah, you saved the day. How ever can I repay you?"

"Live with me," I said. "Happily ever after."

Cooper took my hand, and we bowed for the kids while I tried to hide my grin at the enraptured look on one little girl's face.

When the kids and parents alike burst into applause, we bowed again, though this time I had eyes for Cooper and Cooper alone. Leave it to him to make this the best story time we'd ever had.

But my euphoria only lasted as long as the applause, because it hit me all at once. I wasn't falling in love with Cooper.

I was already flat on the ground, breathless and blinking up at the dark future looming in front of me, wondering how I'd gotten here and what the hell I was going to do now.

Chapter Eighteen

Cooper

"You didn't have to do all this, you know," Corinne murmured as the white-coated waiter stepped away after pushing in her chair. "When you said you wanted to feed me because I stayed at work late, I thought you meant . . . you know, pizza or something. This is a little much for an hour of overtime."

As she eyed me speculatively, I kept my poker face firmly in place.

"I was craving an amazing steak," I said with a shrug as I turned my attention to the wine list. But that was just a cover. After the progress we'd made over the weekend at the charity event, I wasn't about to send myself sliding back down the slippery slope of rejection by pushing too hard.

That said? The idea of a night without her sucked the big one. For a guy who had been sure he'd been in love before, what I felt for Corinne was so much more . . . so all-consuming, I had to wonder now. After a little time away, I'd managed to get a grip on hanging out with my brother Gavin and Emma pretty easily.

But as I read casually through the wine list, my knuckles turned white at the thought of seeing Corinne with another guy.

Never going to happen. If she decided she didn't want me anymore, I'd have to open another branch of the company. Only this time, it would be in Italy. Or maybe Australia. I'd need the distance, because this woman had my heart like no other ever had before.

"I was going to have something light, but now that I see the butter-poached lobster with pea puree, I'm tempted," she murmured, letting out a little groan of pleasure at the thought.

That made my blood race south again as I recalled her making that same sound before, but with much less clothing on.

"Lobster it is," I announced, setting down the menu. "And I think I feel like something bubbly. I'll have the waiter select a champagne for us to go with our appetizers."

As if I'd summoned him with my words, our waiter strolled up, looking sharp in a crisp black jacket, his shoes shined to a high polish. After I ordered, he offered us a warm smile. "Are we celebrating something special, sir?"

I shook my head and grinned. "Just the company of this beautiful woman."

As he scurried away, I realized with a start that this was a celebration of sorts, even if Corinne didn't realize it. We'd made huge strides in our relationship. I was starting to feel like she was actually opening up to me, and it only fed my hunger to know more about her. Share more of myself.

"So, I was thinking the other night about how alike our childhoods were in some ways, and then about the adults we grew up to be," I said, pausing to catch her eye in the candlelight. Damn, was she gorgeous. "I would never wish any of that stuff on a kid, but I wonder who we would be if things had been different."

A busboy dropped off a steaming basket of rolls and filled our water glasses. When he left, Corinne nodded.

"Yeah, I've thought a lot about that myself," she said. "There are definitely parts I would change, but at the same time, I like who I am most times. And I feel like a lot of my drive and determination comes from *not* having . . . if that makes sense. Like, instead of saying, 'I guess this is the way it's going to be,' I took it as a challenge. Most kids in my situation would wind up repeating the cycle, but I refused to accept that fate."

I picked up a roll and set it on her plate, then took one for myself. The waiter came back and poured our champagne, and when he left, she cupped her glass with a shy smile.

"Thank you for this, for tonight. I don't normally go to places like this."

"Anything for you," I murmured.

Her eyes were bright with curiosity as she watched me. "Have you always been a romantic?"

I considered her question. "In a way, I guess I have. I had my first girlfriend at age eight."

"Eight?" Corinne's tone was one of shock.

"Yeah." I chuckled, remembering it. "There was this girl I liked, one of our neighbors. She was ten. Anyway, I told my brothers, and they helped me. They dressed me in a spiffy secondhand suit, bought a heart-shaped box of chocolates, and picked flowers for me to give her. They even helped me write her a poem."

"Oh my." Corinne chuckled. "I would love to hear it."

"Lucky for you, it's etched in my memory for all eternity, so grab hold of your panties so you don't wind up throwing them at me out of pure, unadulterated lust," I warned before clearing my throat. "Roses are red, violets are blue, last night I had a dream, that I was kissing you."

Corinne tossed her head back and let out a belly laugh as I took a sip of my champagne.

"Are you done?" I asked, feigning insult. "Because I thought it was pretty brilliant myself. And it worked, I'll have you know."

"She kissed you for that?" Corinne asked, her eyes widening incredulously.

"Well, no. She kissed me for the chocolates, but still."

For the next two hours, we talked and shared more stories, no encouragement needed. Some were funny, some were sad. But when our luxurious dinner was over, I felt like we'd made even more strides toward becoming ... something else. Something different. Something amazing and life-altering.

I couldn't help but hope tonight would be the night that she came back to my place and stayed. But when I suggested it, Corinne shut down completely, telling me she had to get going and how tired she was.

Once I dropped her off back at the office to pick up her car, I found myself watching her go, feeling lonelier than ever.

Being with Corinne was like a drug. The more I had, the more I craved. The only thing I needed to know was how to make her as addicted to me as I was to her. It was no easy task, considering how hard she was fighting it, but after tonight I was more certain than ever.

She wanted me.

She cared about me.

She might even love me.

But if I wanted her for more than just sex and companionship, I was going to have to be patient.

As she climbed into her car and gave me a little wave, I waved back, a sense of determination settling over me.

It wasn't *good-bye*. It was *see you tomorrow*. Which meant, lucky for me, I had nothing but time on my hands.

Time at work, time after work, weekend functions . . . all opportunities to get her to see how good we were together.

And I was going to milk them for all they were worth.

Chapter Nineteen

Corinne

Saturday was supposed to be an easy day, and it probably was for most people. Unfortunately, my life wasn't like most people's. The entire day had been a shit show. I felt like I'd been running errands for the past six days—it was more like three hours, but still—and I was tired and cranky.

First, there was dry cleaning to drop off, and then prescriptions to pick up and groceries to buy, and now I was running late. I needed to get home and get Aaron loaded up so I could take him to his doctor's appointment. I hadn't run any red lights yet, but I was speeding a good ten miles an hour over every posted speed limit. I hated being late, so I was mumbling silent prayers to myself as I weaved in and out of traffic. Worst of all? I had to pee. That pit stop through the Starbucks drive-through had been my undoing. Hey, a girl had needs.

What had gotten me through my stressful morning? Thoughts of Cooper. I still couldn't believe he'd planned such a romantic date earlier this week. We weren't dating, I mean, we were fucking. There was a difference, right?

But no matter how many times I'd tried to convince Cooper—and myself—that we couldn't be anything more, I always found myself wanting to give him more.

Like his offer for a sleepover. God, I wanted to. The rational part of me knew it wasn't a good idea, but that didn't stop me from wanting it.

After I picked up Aaron, we made it just in time to the doctor's office where he'd get a checkup, and then we'd cover his physical therapy progress. As we stepped into the waiting room, I was surprised to be greeted by four feet, eleven inches of gray-haired sass.

"Mauve?" I squinted, confusion washing over me. "What are you doing here?"

She shrugged. "Got one of the nurses to drop me off on her way home, and promised her that you'd give me a lift back. I'm not an invalid, kiddo. Stop gaping at me like that."

She was right, but still, an outing was a big deal for her. I couldn't quite believe she was here.

"I don't understand. Why did you come?"

She leaned in to give me a one-armed hug. "Because

you shouldn't have to do all of this alone."

She was wrong, but I didn't correct her. I was Aaron's legal guardian. The responsibility of his care did fall on me, but it was nice to have someone notice and understand that sometimes responsibility took a toll.

"Thanks for coming."

Seconds later, Aaron's name was called, and off we went through the wide door and into the doctor's office. We waited in the small interior office, just us three. Aaron looked out at the aquarium that sat against one wall.

As unexpected as her visit was, it was nice to see Mauve outside the walls of the retirement community where she now lived. She'd been a part of my life, and Aaron's, for as long as I could remember, and there was something comforting about the three of us together again, in the same room.

She'd raised Aaron and me as brother and sister, and as close as we all were, she made no qualms about disagreeing with my decisions now that we were older. She saw my relationship with Aaron as a refusal to move on with my life. I saw it as a testament to my loyalty, as a commitment to him.

"What's going on with that man-friend of yours?" Mauve winked.

Ah, there it was. The real reason for her visit today. She wanted to grill me about Cooper.

For just a moment, I imagined telling her everything—every lovely detail about Cooper Kingsley—if only to let myself fantasize that I was a normal twenty-something woman with a normal love life. But reality came crashing down on me as the harsh fluorescent lights reminded me of our surroundings. Best not to encourage her.

"There's nothing to tell. It's nothing, Mauve. I made an oath to Aaron. End of story."

She squared her shoulders. "Yes, you did. And I know you'll never break it, that you'll never toss him to the wayside. But he'd want you to move on with your life. It doesn't mean Aaron won't be a part of it, but he shouldn't be the only part. He'd want you to have a husband, children, big family Christmases, all the things you two dreamed about."

I swallowed hard, blinking back tears.

"You know why that's so hard to hear?"

I glared at her. "No, but I bet you're going to tell me."

A coy smile graced her lips. "It's because I'm right, kiddo."

The medical assistant chose that moment to enter the room, thank God, and I stole away for a few moments while she checked Aaron's vitals. I needed to get away from Mauve's judging eyes, and I seriously still needed to pee.

After locating the restroom, I relieved myself and washed my hands.

When my eyes met my reflection, the woman looking back at me was unfamiliar. She was more confident, for one. I couldn't quite put my finger on what it was. The set of my shoulders, the tilt of my chin, maybe.

As much as I didn't want to admit it to myself, this affair with Cooper had been good for me. I never did things like this, things that were just for me. My cheeks were flushed pink, and my eyes glistened with anticipation.

An idea struck me, and feeling almost giddy, I quickly pulled my phone from my purse. I punched in Cooper's name and began a new text.

> *Is that offer for a sleepover still good?*

I didn't expect his reply so quickly, and was about to shove my phone back into my purse when three little dots appeared, letting me know he was composing his message.

> *Of course it is. But it's not nice to tease a man, dove.*

I wasn't nervous—not really. This was Cooper. I knew he'd be careful, knew he'd take control so I didn't have to think, and that was what I craved.

I was tired of being in charge. My personal life was chaotic, and I craved his complete domination. I wanted to shut off my brain and just enjoy myself for once, without having to rush home after. I knew I could pay Tabitha extra to spend the night with Aaron, and so really nothing was standing in my way.

> *Me + you . . . all night long. Think you can handle that?*

I could almost see him smirking down at his phone with that trademark half smile he had. That playful side to him that I loved.

Fuck yes, I can. Tell me when.

I have to work out the best night, but soon.

Cooper had begged me to stay over so many times, and I loved how happy I knew this would make him.

And, Coop? I swallowed down a wave of nerves and typed out the rest of my message. *I promise I'll tell you everything very soon.*

I trust you.

His reply stung deep in my chest.

I hadn't earned his trust, not with the colossal secret I'd been keeping from him. But we were growing closer than ever, and the hard truth I'd kept from him this entire time was going to come out. And when it did, I had a feeling it would ruin everything.

Trying not to think about that just yet, I shoved my phone in my purse and headed back to the exam room.

Chapter Twenty

Cooper

"I think that's every blanket in the place," I said as I set the pile onto the cushioned outdoor sofa before pulling the sliding glass door shut.

"You really didn't have to do that," Corinne replied, but even as she spoke, I could see snuggling in closer against the cool air.

"Nope, you wanted to spend some time on the balcony. We're going to do it right." I flicked on the outdoor fireplace and waited as the flame sprang to life, then grabbed the nearest blanket and tucked Corinne into the flannel, wrapping her tight like a burrito.

She sat with a happy sigh and grinned up at me. "Why do you have so many blankets? I thought guys didn't really, you know, get into throws and decorative stuff like that." She snuggled deeper against the cushions before sticking a hand out to snatch a second blanket and layer it over herself.

Seeing her face lit with happiness warmed me, and I took one of the throws for myself and settled in beside her.

"Well, to me, they're sort of sentimental. When my mom was home, she had one specific fake-fur blanket she always used, even in the summertime. It was like her comfort object. When she was stressed, she'd sit on the couch and burrow in. It always seemed to help. Sometimes, when we'd had a rough day, she would lift the corner up in an invitation to climb in next to her. Brings back some rare good memories."

"That's sweet," Corinne murmured.

I nodded. "Hers wore out, got all patchy and full of holes before she finally got rid of it. I got her a new one for Christmas a few years later, and she cried." I let out a little chuckle, remembering the way she'd hugged the blanket close to her before kissing my forehead.

Mom wasn't perfect. Far from it, but who was? She was a good woman deep down, and in a very bad situation. It had taken me years to come to terms with that.

"Anyway," I said, shaking myself of the memory, "I keep them around because I like to have little reminders of what life was like back then. It keeps me from taking the here and now for granted."

"It must have been hard. Growing up like that."

Corinne said the words simply enough, but I could feel the weight of her gaze as she surveyed me from beneath her thick lashes.

I nodded. "It was." There was no point in sugarcoating it. I wanted to know her, and in turn, I wanted her to know me. "There are a lot of things I wish I could change. But in some ways, it's helped me learn what's important. What I want for my life."

She turned to face me now, her face washed in the flickering orange firelight. "And what is it that you want?"

"You don't already know the answer?" I raised my eyebrows as she shook her head.

"I want love," I said, shrugging. "Balls to the wall, totally uninhibited love. I want all of it. I think you do too, even if you won't admit it."

She stared at me for a long moment as my heart thudded in my chest. This wasn't part of our agreement; I knew that. Just like I knew she could get up and walk out the door at any moment.

But I was through being careful. I'd handed my heart

over more than once because I wanted to believe I'd been in that kind of love. No fucking way was I going to hold back now that I'd actually found it. Not anymore.

The breath was suspended in my lungs as I waited to see if she would run. But she sat there regarding me, her expressive eyes filled with fear mixed with something else, and it made my heart thrum.

"I know that wasn't our arrangement." I pressed on, my heartbeat thundering in my ears. "But I want you to know where I stand. I want all of you, Corinne."

Slowly, she wet her lips with the tip of her tongue, a sadness shadowing her face.

"I can't give that to you, and someday I'll explain why. But . . ." Her voice quavered and she started again. "But I want to. Does that count for anything, Cooper? I want to so badly."

I hadn't scaled her walls yet, but damn it, I'd knocked them down a few stories. For now, I'd take it.

The time for talking was done. I needed to claim her, to take her to my bed and show her what she meant to me. Taking her by the hand, I led her inside. Wordlessly, she followed me to my bedroom.

In the pale moonlight streaming through the windows, we fell onto the bed together, kissing and groping. My cock rutted uselessly against her belly until she finally drew it out, stroking me with her delicate hands.

"That feels so nice, sweetheart." I peppered her lush mouth with kisses as she stroked me.

Pushing my fingers under the elastic of her panties, I brought her to orgasm while we kissed. By then, my cock was so hard and achy, I couldn't wait any longer.

"Come here, baby." I urged Corinne into my lap.

She smiled shyly and leaned down to kiss me, her mouth moving from my lips down to my neck. The thought of fucking her from behind had been on my mind since I first caught sight of all her luscious curves.

"Turn around."

I wanted to push her, wanted to continue to watch her grow and blossom under my instruction. And so far, we'd only made love in the missionary position. It was time to change things up.

Corinne hesitated for a moment, but then she moved

to straddle me.

I shook my head. "Facing my feet."

The technical term was reverse cowgirl, but I had a feeling that might scare her off. I was sure that despite her growing confidence in the bedroom, those words might conjure images of a cowgirl riding a rodeo bull, and I wanted her to feel relaxed, not under the spotlight, like she was expected to perform for me. And truly, she wasn't. She could have laid like a log under me during sex and it still would have been amazing, but this was about growth, about pushing her ever so subtly outside her comfort zone.

She paused, kneeling beside me on the bed. "I—I won't know what I'm doing."

I touched her shoulder. "That's my job to worry about. I'll show you what I like, what will feel good for both of us."

"I don't know."

If it weren't for the spark of curiosity in her eyes, I wouldn't have pushed for this at all. I would have just let it drop and gone back to missionary, which we both enjoyed. Immensely.

"It's a shame to be blessed with an ass like that and not let me see you work it." My voice was gruff, raw, but it was the challenge in my words that must have undone her resolve.

Corinne smiled and climbed into my lap, facing away from me like I'd instructed. "Show me how to make you lose your mind, Cooper," she whispered, her voice low and sultry.

My cock jumped as it made contact with the lush curves of her ass. "Gladly, dove."

Chapter Twenty-One

Corinne

I'd given him everything. I hadn't meant to, of course. But Cooper owned every part of my body, my soul, my thoughts, my smiles, and even my heart—even though I'd promised us both that could never happen.

The truth was I'd fallen for him, desperately. And worst of all? He still didn't know the truth.

I hated myself that I'd let things get this far, that I'd never grown a pair and actually told him, explained the whole sordid mess like Mauve had encouraged I do.

"Corinne?" Alyssa's voice cut through my thoughts. "Are you okay?"

I nodded, pretending I was focused on something on my computer screen. "Of course. Why?"

I attempted a smile, but it felt wrong on my lips. My stomach was queasy and my palms were sweaty. If Alyssa thought something was wrong, Cooper would know in an instant. He'd read me like a book from day one. Best to avoid him today.

Alyssa's features scrunched up in disbelief. "Because

I asked you three times if you want to try that new sushi place for lunch, and it was like you were far away or something."

"Sushi sounds great. Sorry, I was trying to get through these invoices."

Thankfully, she nodded and didn't press me further, which was rather unlike Alyssa. Normally, she was like a dog with a bone, but maybe something in my solemn expression told her to leave it alone. And for once, she did.

We worked in silence and later went to lunch together, where she kept the conversation flowing about the semi-annual sale she'd shopped over the weekend, updating her wardrobe for a steal. I was only half listening, shoveling bites of cucumber roll into my mouth, even though I wasn't hungry. In fact, it was a wonder I got anything down at all. My nerves were shot.

As I sat there in the bustling sushi bar, one thing became abundantly clear. I had to cut Cooper from my life. One quick, clean slice. Rip off the Band-Aid. Sure, it would be painful at first, heart-wrenching even, but as the months passed, I felt confident Cooper and I would fall into a rhythm again as boss and employee, and nothing more.

It was the safest thing to do for everyone involved.

My phone buzzed in my hip pocket, and I pulled it out, revealing Cooper's name. Ignoring his call, I went back to nodding along to whatever Alyssa was saying.

Chapter Twenty-Two

Cooper

"Corinne called out sick again."

"What do you mean?" I demanded, but Alyssa only blinked back at me.

"She said she's not coming in. Whatever she's got must really be bad."

I tightened my jaw, trying to tamp down the wave of nausea that rolled through me. "I'll say. That's the fourth day in a row. Anyway, thanks, Alyssa. You need me to get you a temp to pick up the slack?"

"Nope, I'm good," she said with a sympathetic smile. "Just thought you'd want to know."

Alyssa stepped from my office and closed the door softly behind her just in time for me to let out a low breath. I couldn't understand it.

Calling out of work was one thing. People got sick. But there was something else going on here, something far worse. Corinne had stopped responding to my calls and messages. And now she wasn't coming into work, either?

Those were some serious hoops to jump through to avoid me, which she was definitely doing. But what I couldn't understand was *why*.

Our night together on Saturday had been ... well, beyond amazing. I'd thought about it nearly every free second I had all week, and even some I didn't. It consumed my thoughts. Her body had been so yielding and soft, so willing and responsive, and when I'd slid into her, I knew that she wanted it as much as I did. Not just the sex but the intimacy, the closeness we'd been working toward these past weeks. I wasn't delusional. She was feeling all the same things I felt.

But it hadn't stopped her from slipping out in the morning before I'd woken up.

Spearing a hand through my hair, I shook my head and blew out a sigh. Was it something I'd said? I supposed I could have scared her with my declaration of intent, with my need to be with her. But she'd said she wanted that too.

That she couldn't have it, but she *wanted* it.

And what did that even mean? She was a young, beautiful woman with her whole life ahead of her. What was holding her back? I knew, of course, about what had happened when she was in foster care, but if that was what she needed to work through, I would go to counseling with her. I would do anything I could to make it right between us, and by now she had to know that.

So, there was something else, something beyond a fear of commitment. There had to be.

The workday dragged by, and I felt frustrated and more uneasy with each passing hour. By the time five o'clock rolled around, I couldn't sit still any longer. I stepped from my office and made my way down the hall toward Quinn's door. I knocked, and when there was no answer, I opened the door to find his office empty.

My stomach squirmed with the slightest trace of guilt, but I made my way toward the filing cabinet all the same. Opening the drawer for personnel, I thumbed my way to the manila folder with Corinne's name on it.

Like with all the core staff, I'd read her résumé when she was first hired, but I looked it over again, trying to find some clue of what she might be hiding. All the details of her schooling and prior employment checked out with what she'd told me. There were some awards and training she'd never mentioned, but that was normal.

Sighing, I set the sheets down on Quinn's desk, ready to resign myself to the mystery once and for all, when another piece of paper slipped out of the file folder. I bent low to pick it up and spied Corinne's neat cursive writing, stark blue against the white sheet, a medical insurance form.

I glanced at it briefly, ready to slide it back where it belonged. But before I got the chance, I caught sight of something that sucked the air from my lungs.

Two little boxes rocked my whole world. One empty, one checked off.

For a second, my brain couldn't comprehend what I was seeing, and then it became all too real.

Corinne was married.

My head reeling, I glanced lower and found her spouse's information filled in with that same tidy handwriting.

Aaron O'Neil.

Her roommate.

The man she'd been so desperate that I should never

meet. The person she refused to discuss. He was her fucking husband.

Sucking in my cheeks, I shoved the papers back in the file and slammed the metal drawer closed, my heart surging in my chest.

"Aaron fucking O'Neil," I muttered through gritted teeth.

But it wasn't enough to rage quietly to myself. I had to make sure she knew what I now knew myself—that she understood what she'd done to me. How, without even trying, she'd made me fall in love with a woman I could never have.

"Son of a bitch," I murmured under my breath, stalking from my brother's office and making my way back to my own sanctuary. Slamming the door behind me, I ripped my cell phone from my pocket and scrolled to Corinne's number.

Beneath the series of unanswered messages I'd left, I added a new one.

You're. Fucking. Married.

I typed every letter with all the force I could muster

before hitting SEND and shutting the phone off. Let her sit with what she'd done for a while. Let her know what it felt like to be ignored and avoided.

I was through.

What a fucking idiot. God, how many times was I going to let someone do this to me?

But as much as I tried to compare Corinne to the other women I'd loved, I knew the truth. There would be no bouncing back from this one. No searching for love again. Corinne had broken me.

Within a matter of seconds, my door opened and Gavin appeared, his brows knit together. "What's going on? Did you mean to slam your door? I—"

"She's married," I choked out, raking a hand through my hair.

"What?" Gavin took another step inside the room before shutting the door after himself.

"Corinne. She's fucking married."

"What?" He blinked. "Are you serious? You can't—"

"It was right there under our noses." I slammed a hand against my desk. "She put him on her medical insurance and everything. How did none of us notice that?"

Gavin shook his head. "How could we have known? Benefits handles all that, and I wasn't about to tell them you were sleeping with one of our employees. We would have been crazy to even think—"

"Except we didn't think. And she is. Fucking married." I gritted my teeth again and scrubbed a hand over my stubbled jaw. "She's been avoiding me. Talking about how she wants to be with me but she can't, and now I know why. She's using me to cheat on her poor fucking husband."

Gavin took a deep breath. "Look, let me call Quinn. We'll bounce early and spend some time at my place. If you want, I can tell Emma to go out with her friends for a while and—"

"Don't bother. I'm not going to kick your wife out of her own home. It's all right if she's there. I just need to blow off some steam."

I gathered up my things and followed him out of the office, my guts churning as we got into his town car.

Once the driver pulled the car onto the street, Gavin

sent a quick text, then reached for the bottle of whiskey he always kept in the icebox. Taking one of the cut crystal glasses from the shelf beside him, he poured a healthy measure and then handed it to me.

"Drink," he commanded.

"I don't want to drink," I said. In fact, I didn't want to do much of anything except find Aaron O'Neil and apologize for sleeping with his wife.

God, what a nightmare I'd gotten myself into. And all because I hadn't learned my lesson the first time. This was what I got for letting my heart guide me.

Never again.

"I didn't ask if you wanted to drink. I told you to drink. We're going to handle this the way Kingsley men do. With alcohol and self-loathing." He poured himself his own glass, then clinked it to mine before taking a swig.

It wouldn't solve anything, but right now, I was willing to go along. Anything to dull the throbbing pain in my chest where my heart used to be. I followed suit, swallowing hard as the liquid burned its way down my throat.

"So, what do I do?" I asked after the last of my drink

was gone.

"What have you already done?" Gavin asked.

"I texted her and told her I knew . . . in not so many words."

"And where is your phone now?"

I sighed. "I left it at the office. I just can't deal with that right now. I don't want to hear her excuses."

"Good decision. Tonight, we're going to let boys be boys, okay?"

We pulled up in front of Gavin's high-rise and made our way quickly to the penthouse. When we stepped inside, we found Emma and Quinn already there, sitting in the sunken living room, chatting quietly about something I couldn't hear.

Based on their expressions when they turned to look at me, though, I had a pretty good guess.

Emma stood instantly before sweeping across the room and kissing her husband on the cheek. "Hey," she said, then moved toward me and kissed me on the cheek too.

"Hi." My voice sounded gritty. "Nice to see you."

And it was. In spite of everything we'd been through, when I looked at her now, I felt . . . well, nothing. I loved her, yes, but only because she loved my brother and took care of him.

Because now that I'd been with Corinne?

I knew what love actually felt like. What it was to want to be with a person so badly that you could hardly breathe when they weren't around.

The truth was I'd never felt that way about Emma. I'd found her attractive and interesting and kind, but she didn't light me on fire the way Corinne did. She didn't make me want to stay up all night peppering her with questions just so I had a little more of her to carry with me throughout our moments apart.

Emma squeezed my bicep. "I was going to order pizza, and then I'll give you guys some space. Have a favorite topping?"

"Don't let him pick. He's an anchovy guy," Quinn said.

"Then he'll get his own pizza with extra anchovies." Emma grinned. "Sound good?"

I nodded and she slipped from the room, her cell

phone in hand, leaving me alone with my brothers.

Quinn stood up and made his way to the bar cart. Without asking, he poured three measures of Gavin's best bourbon and held them out to us. If Gavin minded, he didn't say as much.

"So, there's no need to tell me what happened. Gavin took care of that," Quinn said. "Tonight, we don't even have to talk about it if you don't want to."

"I don't know what there is to talk about." I took a seat on the sofa. "She's married. I can't be with her now. Even if she did leave her husband, how could I ever trust her?"

Quinn nodded, then took a sip of his drink. "I know."

I turned to Gavin. "You should tell Emma she doesn't have to hide. I don't mind if she's around."

Gavin shook his head. "I know that. I just think it's better if it's the three of us tonight. Now come on, let's drink like we mean it."

Quinn clinked his glass to Gavin's and the three of us settled in, discussing business, sports … anything and everything except for the state of my love life.

I knew they were trying to distract me, and sometimes I did find myself laughing or talking about the old times. But more often than not, my mind would drift back to Corinne. When it did, I'd take another sip, wishing I could quiet my racing thoughts.

It was good not to be alone, but even surrounded by my brothers, I felt isolated. My heart was shattered in ways they could never understand, and even though they tried, there was no way of explaining this to them. No way of feeling truly whole.

So I drank and ate pizza and played along, finally passing out a little after midnight, but I knew when morning came I would feel the same.

Broken and beyond repair.

Tomorrow I would be well and truly alone in this. Reality would finally sink in, and I'd be facing a life without the only woman I'd ever truly loved.

Motherfucker.

Chapter Twenty-Three

Corinne

After Monday, I didn't go to work for the rest of the week. At first, it had been out of my own stupid self-hatred and pity. I couldn't face Cooper, not after everything we'd shared. Because, in truth, the second I saw him again, I knew I'd sneak into his office and beg for more. I was crazy about him—ready to change my entire life and all my commitments just to make room for him.

I wanted every bit of him, all his happiness and sadness, his light and his dark, just like he wanted those things from me. *Some* just wasn't enough anymore.

Which, of course, was exactly why I needed the space. In the first few days, I'd looked for a new job, but every time I thought about going to work and not seeing Cooper and Alyssa and all the people who'd so quickly become a respite from my stressful life, I couldn't bring myself to schedule the interviews.

Then, feeling lost and unsure, I spent Friday with Mauve, pouring out my heart only to get the same answer in return—this wasn't what Aaron would have wanted for my life. I needed to do what made me happy, and more than anything, I needed to find a way to tell the truth.

My head spinning, I'd left the retirement home that night and flicked on my phone to find a message from Cooper. That in itself wasn't so unusual, though. I'd been fending him off for days. No, it was the content of the message that made my heart stop beating and my breath catch.

You're. Fucking. Married.

It wasn't a question, and I couldn't answer it like one. My throat went dry and my fingers trembled over the keyboard as I tapped out my reply.

I can explain.

I sent the message, but knowing that could never be enough, I added, *Can we meet for coffee tomorrow morning?*

But by the time morning came, despite my checking every five minutes through that sleepless night, there was still no answer. I spent the day by Aaron's side, trying to think of all the best ways to explain why I did what I'd done, and how I planned to make it right. But even then, with all the options in the world available to me, one look at Aaron brought me crashing back to reality.

No matter what happened with Cooper, even if I did

get him to understand all my lies and deception, nothing was going to make this okay. Nothing would make my life normal and whole and complete, not without hurting someone I cared for deeply and needed me.

On Saturday night, an answer finally dinged on my phone. Cooper had written simple instructions to meet him at a coffee shop at nine the next morning. The place was close to the office, and even though I knew nothing good could come of it and it might be the last time I ever saw his face, my heart still swelled with the idea of seeing him again.

• • •

When Sunday dawned, I dressed quickly and carefully, making sure to feed Aaron and give him his medication before I slipped out the door.

The whole way to the coffee shop, I nervously combed my fingers through my hair, imagining the long wait for Cooper before he finally arrived. It was only eight thirty, but I couldn't bring myself to wait another minute.

Still, when I reached the little outdoor seating area that led into the main shop, I saw that Cooper was already sitting there, his eyes downcast as he surveyed the morning paper. A steaming cup of coffee sat in front of him, and as he reached for it, his gaze met mine, and I caught sight of the days of stubble along his jaw.

My heart stuttered, and I reminded myself to breathe as I took another shaky step toward him.

I'd never seen him dressed this way. He wore faded jeans and a sweatshirt, a ball cap covering his head, and he looked exhausted. A shell of himself. Like a balloon that all the air had been let out of.

With another jagged breath, I realized I was the one who'd done this to him.

Blinking back hot tears I didn't deserve to shed, I hitched my bag higher on my shoulder, then took the seat across from him before folding my hands on the table between us.

He sipped his coffee, his gaze never wavering from mine, though he made no motion to greet me. A waitress appeared and I ordered quickly, watching her retreat before finally clearing my throat to speak.

"I'm sure you have questions." I'd practiced my opening statement a million times in my mind, but hearing the words made them hollower than I'd ever imagined.

Still, I pressed on as he raised his eyebrows. "Before I answer them, though, I want to tell you things as they are from my perspective."

He made no motion to argue. In fact, as far as I could tell, he was barely breathing. So, without a lifeline, I forced myself to continue.

"I met Aaron when I was young. We grew up in the same shelter, and once, we were even placed in the same foster home for a little while." I chewed my bottom lip. "I've thought about how to explain this for days, and I still can't seem to find the words to express what the constancy of his presence meant for me. When I was placed in a new home, I always had someone I could call who would console me about the new people or share in my small and infrequent triumphs. He was my best friend—my only friend, really—and as we got older, it was natural that our relationship changed too."

Cooper gripped his coffee mug and brought it to his lips, his knuckles white as he gripped the handle.

I swallowed hard. "Anyway, he was my first kiss. My best friend. My family. I couldn't imagine my life without him, and we promised each other we'd always be together, in one way or another."

Cooper let the cup clatter back onto its saucer, his jaw tightening. "This is what you just had to tell me? How you and your husband are fucking soulmates?" He let out a low snort, his eyes flat with fury. "Do you want to make it easier and just shove a knife in my back or what?"

I drew back, both stung and sick with guilt. "Please, hear me out." I rushed on, desperate to make him understand. "I know this part is hard to hear, but it's important, okay?"

He let out a sigh but didn't get up and leave, which was all the permission I needed.

"Anyway, we aged out of the system at eighteen, and so decided to get an apartment together. Aaron woke up late for work that particular morning. He tore out of the apartment, hopped on his bike, and tried to race his way there. In the suburbs, though, there aren't many bike lanes, and one blind turn changed both our lives forever. A car plowed directly into him."

Cooper flinched but his expression stayed icy. I pushed on, refusing to let myself get sidetracked from telling the whole truth.

"He'd been saving up for a ring. I knew that, and although I cared about him, things between us were already changing. I was realizing what I felt was love and friendship, but I also knew he wanted more. I planned to talk to him. Break things off. We'd never been intimate, never were lovers in that way." I thumbed the bare space on my ring finger. "Anyway, when the accident happened and I learned the full extent of his injuries, I knew what I had to do."

"What were the full extent of his injuries?"

Cooper's voice startled me for a moment, but I nodded.

"He had a severe head injury. Since he was late for work, he hadn't taken the time to grab his helmet. There was some spinal damage that restricts him to a wheelchair, but the primary issue was the brain damage. He has the mentality of an eight-year-old, and he will for the rest of his life."

Tears burned in the back of my throat, but I pushed past them for Cooper's sake. Today, this story wasn't about Aaron and me. I'd grieved for Aaron for years and always would. Right now, it was about Cooper.

"So, as I was saying, when I knew all that, I understood what I had to do. He was my best friend, and I was all he had in the world, just like he was all I had. Things didn't turn out the way we'd hoped, but I couldn't just give up on him."

The waitress reappeared with my coffee and I took it, grateful to have something to distract me, if only for a moment. Silently, I waited as Cooper processed everything I'd said, sipping my latte, and then he looked up at me with tense, firm lips.

"That must have been devastating for you," he said, his voice low and tight.

"It was a long time ago now. But yes, it was a hard time. I made the decision that we marry. He never asked, but I knew it was what he wanted. Being married . . . well, it meant I would be his caregiver, his legal guardian, and that he'd be covered under my health insurance." I paused, drawing a deep breath.

"Corinne . . ."

Cooper reached a hand toward me, but I didn't take it. Instead, I focused on my coffee, getting out the last of what I'd planned to say.

"Look, I know you must think I'm a horrible person. I am a horrible person. I mean, I've been sleeping with you, a man who isn't my husband, for the past month."

"You're not a bad person." Cooper's voice was soft now, understanding. "You have needs just like anyone else."

"Even though I'm not with Aaron romantically, I still tried to be faithful. About five years ago, I got drunk at a bar and had a one-night stand, but before you . . . before you, I hadn't been touched in many years. I'd slept with two men for a grand total of twice, so all this, with you? It's all still very new to me, and I know now that it was wrong."

Cooper shook his head, his expression softening. "No, Corinne. You're amazing for caring for Aaron this way for so long. I never knew him, but I can't imagine he would want you to lay down your entire life like this. Do you think he would want you to sacrifice everything for him?"

"You sound like Mauve," I said and let out a humorless laugh.

"There's something I still don't understand, though,"

Cooper said.

"What's that?"

"You said you guys were married. How did you . . . Was there a ceremony?"

I nodded. "Aaron didn't have health insurance at the time, so there was a rush to get it done. I had the ceremony performed in his hospital bed. His care is still incredibly expensive, but back then, it was just insane. I didn't buy us rings or anything; it wasn't a romantic gesture. I just needed to be sure that I could take care of him like I needed to."

Cooper nodded. "I understand."

A beat of silence passed between us, and though I wanted to study his face, to try to understand how he was processing all this, I remained transfixed by the mug in front of me. After pouring out my heart to him, I didn't have any energy left to see the hurt or confusion on his face.

"So, what now?" Cooper's voice was deep and thoughtful.

I shrugged. "I don't know. We can't really be together, not in any real way. We can never be more than this."

"Corinne—"

I shook my head, cutting him short. "This is why I tried to find the right words before. See, before Aaron, I had nobody and nothing. Without me, he has nobody and nothing. After everything we went through together, I can never leave him. And I won't divorce him." A tear slid down my cheek, and I swiped it away with the back of my hand. "You have to believe me when I tell you how sorry I am for not being honest with you from the beginning. You should have known everything, even if this was never meant to be serious. It was wrong of me to lie to you."

Cooper shook his head. "I forgive you. Really, I do. I just . . . I don't want to say good-bye."

"We have to." I choked out the words. "This—you and me—we can't be casual lovers. You wouldn't be happy, and I would always want more. I can't spend my time neglecting Aaron when I'm with you, and wishing I was with you when I'm with Aaron. We just can't work."

"So that's it?" Cooper asked dully, and for the first time, I truly knew the answer.

"Yes. I'm so, so sorry."

He leaned across the table and kissed my cheek, his face pale and stark with grief. "Then good-bye, little dove."

Another hot tear rolled down my cheek, and I swiped it away before jumping from my chair and dashing from the café.

Chapter Twenty-Four

Cooper

I blinked my eyes open to find the sun already halfway in the sky, its rays streaming through my sliding glass terrace door to taunt me.

"Shit." I groaned and then rolled over until I fell off the edge of my leather couch and landed ass first on the floor. My head bumped against the side table, and I rubbed it before sitting up and glancing at the clock.

It was almost noon, making this the third day in a row I had not only opted not to work, but had also chosen not to bother calling my brothers to let them know as much.

No doubt they were near murderous about it by now, but I still couldn't summon the energy to care. Instead, I lay back on the carpet and surveyed the mass of beer bottles on my coffee table, counting the little brown circles from beneath the glass table's surface.

Twelve. Which, admittedly, wasn't so bad considering they'd spanned three days of nonstop drinking. The empty bottle of whiskey was somewhat less encouraging, though.

Rolling on my side, I found my phone where I'd left it nearly three days ago.

After all, even without checking, I knew there would be no messages from Corinne. And if there were? It would only be details about when her last day on the job would be.

When my life without her would truly begin.

Fuck.

I couldn't understand how I'd done this again—fallen in love with a woman who would never choose me, no matter the circumstance.

And when I wasn't lying on my couch trying to imagine a world when my every waking thought wasn't about the one woman who made me realize what love really was, I was drifting off to sleep, dreaming of having her in my arms again.

They were simple dreams, so close to reality that they shook me to my core. Made me wake up full of hope and happiness until I realized that they were only dreams.

We were sitting on the terrace, snuggling by the fire, or she was lying spent and sated in my arms after a round of passionate lovemaking. Our conversations were nothing deep or spectacular, but in my mind, they were so real. Like I could wake up and text her to continue the conversation, and she would know exactly what I meant.

But it was all in my head, and I would wake up back in a world where she'd been ripped away from me again. Where I had to remember all over again that I would never have her here with me. That she could never truly be mine.

I pushed a hand through my hair, then scrubbed my hand over my beard just as my phone lit up. I turned to look at it, watching as it vibrated its way across the floor, the ringtone blaring its overly cheery melody. Not that I would bother to see who was calling.

Instead, just like I had the million other times this had happened, I got to my feet and ignored it, grabbing a blanket from my bedroom before returning to the couch for another round of much-needed sleep.

Eventually, I would be able to wake up and look at all my messages. I'd have to.

But that day wasn't today. For now, I was going to wallow until the hole in my chest felt a little bit smaller.

Snuggling onto the leather cushions, I pulled my

knees close to my chest and wrapped the blanket around me before closing my eyes and trying desperately to focus on something, anything, that didn't remind me of Corinne.

Still, as I drifted off, her face appeared again, smiling at something I couldn't remember saying, and she was laughing. Then I was laughing too and—

My heart stopped as something pounded hard and loud against my front door. I blinked, jumping to my feet.

"Cooper!" Gavin's yell was muffled by the door, but I would know his voice anywhere.

"Go away," I shouted back.

"Open this fucking door, you dick," Quinn commanded, and I held my breath as they began to pound again.

"We're not leaving until you let us inside," Gavin added, and I knew he'd be true to his word.

Seeing no other option, I padded toward the door and opened it, turning my back on my brothers before making my way back to my couch and flopping back onto the cushions.

"Jesus," Gavin said as he surveyed the rows of empty bottles while Quinn scooped my phone from the floor and sat it in front of me. "You're a real fucking mess, yeah?"

"What do you need?" I asked none too politely.

Quinn took a seat on the sofa opposite me and crossed his arms over his barrel of a chest. "I want to know what's going on. I haven't seen you this bad, even when—" He stopped short as Gavin winced.

"You can say it. I don't care," I said.

"Fine, then. Since Emma." Quinn nodded. "The last we heard from you, you were going to talk to Corinne, then you just don't show up for work and don't answer anyone's calls? Do you know how that made us feel? We were half expecting to find you dead."

Gavin nodded, then took a seat beside our older brother. "Look, we know this is hard for you. We just want to know what happened so we can help. Corinne resigned."

I nodded. "I thought she might. So she's already gone, then?"

Quinn didn't bother answering, but his mouth flattened into a thin line.

"Today's her last day," Gavin said. "Just tell us what happened. We only want to help."

So I did. I told them about how I'd gone to the coffee shop and listened as the woman I loved described her deep and unmovable love for another man. About my devastation and heartbreak over her loss and tragedy. And about what she'd said when her story was over—about how she could never share her heart with both Aaron and me.

Both my brothers were quiet for a long moment after I'd finished, but Quinn clasped his hands together, staring at them as he spoke slowly and carefully. "I'm sorry about all of that, Cooper. I really am."

Gavin nodded. "It's a raw deal."

I let out a humorless laugh. "At this point, I think I should just learn to expect this kind of thing. As soon as I have feelings for someone, I should just assume they can never be with me."

Quinn tilted his head to the side. "Don't be dramatic."

"Can you blame me?" I demanded. "I've had a pretty fucked year, bro."

Quinn let out a breath. "I guess not. Still, there's one thing about Corinne's story I can't puzzle out."

"What's that?" I asked.

He spread his hands wide. "If Aaron was as brain damaged and injured as she says, how could he have been in the right frame of mind to consent to a marriage? It doesn't make sense. He couldn't have recited the vows or signed the marriage license."

Gavin's face lit up. "Yeah, that makes sense. How could that be legal?"

I sighed. "You're not getting it. Legal or not, this guy is her husband. She won't leave him."

Quinn fished out his phone and started typing furiously while Gavin surveyed me from the couch.

"So, she loves this guy like a brother, though, right? She doesn't have romantic feelings for him?"

"Right." I nodded. "But that doesn't matter."

"I'm not so sure about that." Gavin shrugged, but before he could continue, Quinn looked back up at both of us.

"Coop, there's no way her marriage is legally binding. I'll do some more intensive research, but everything I'm seeing so far says that it can't possibly be."

"And ten minutes of research gave you the ultimate answer?" I scoffed.

Quinn rolled his eyes. "Like I said, I'm going to keep looking, but there's hope here."

"I don't know about that." Hope was the worst thing, the thing that would truly be the nail in my coffin. And still . . . I wanted to believe him with every ounce of my being.

Gavin pursed his lips. "I think you're giving up on this too easily. Don't you think there could be room for all three of you in this relationship? In some fashion, at least?"

"What do you mean?" I asked.

"Just think about it, okay?" Quinn said. "I'll send you all the information I can find, but you need to do some soul searching too."

"Preferably without these." Gavin motioned to the

empty bottles littering the coffee table.

"Right," I said. "I'll work on that."

Together, Gavin and Quinn got up from the couch and made their way back to the door.

"Call us if you're going to miss work again," Quinn said, and then they were gone, leaving me alone with my thoughts.

Sitting back on the couch, I glanced down at my baggy hoodie and sweatpants. They were right. I had to do some soul searching, and there was no chance of me making any progress with that here.

I was going to take a shower, and then I'd hunt down the one person who knew Corinne best.

Mauve.

Chapter Twenty-Five

Cooper

"My goodness, aren't you handsome?" Mauve said, looking me up and down.

"Thank you." I smirked. She wouldn't have thought so an hour ago. The shower and shave I'd made time for had been essential.

"This is about Corinne, yes?" The old woman staring at me was smiling so hard, I thought her dentures might fall out.

"I was hoping to get your ..." *What? Blessing?* "Insight," I finally settled on.

With her eyes still crinkling in the corners, she pointed to the chair next to her bed. "Sit. Let's figure it out."

I followed her instructions, already amused by her. Some part of my brain recognized that she'd been waiting for this moment and was glad it was finally here.

I took a deep breath. "Yes, this is about Corinne. I'm in love with her."

There was something about talking to an elderly

person that removed your need for a filter. I didn't know if I felt freer to speak because I sensed deep down that she didn't have much time left, or because I knew that none of the pleasantries were needed. Life was too short not to go after what you wanted. And I definitely wanted Corinne.

"That's wonderful, Cooper. She's told me how much you mean to her too. That's why she ran."

"I'm sorry?"

"Aaron. She uses him as a crutch. She's terrified of love. She's never been loved and cherished the way she deserved to be her entire life. It's made her fearful."

Several things struck me at once. First, I'd been a fucking idiot. How could I not have seen that Corinne was using Aaron? Maybe their marriage wasn't legally binding, but that wasn't enough to explain her actions. She was scared.

"What if you left her? What if you hurt her?" Mauve smoothed the thin cotton blanket over her legs. "Aaron would never do that."

I nodded, understanding for the first time that asking Corinne to try a relationship with me was the most terrifying thing she could imagine. "So, what do I do?"

Mauve offered me a sad smile. "That depends. Can you handle there being another man in your relationship?"

I thought about it for half a second, and opened my mouth to respond.

Mauve held up a hand, stopping me. "He'll need around-the-clock care, and there are doctors' appointments and physical therapy, and . . ."

I shook my head to stop her. She wasn't going to talk me out of this. "I understand that. And I am prepared—financially and emotionally."

Mauve smiled again. "Then what are you doing sitting around talking to me for? Go get your girl."

Quinn had said today was Corinne's last day at the office. I checked my phone for the time. It was late in the afternoon. She might already be gone.

With a flash of nerves, I hopped up from my chair, kissed Mauve's cheek, and all but ran out of the retirement home to the parking lot.

Speeding the entire way to the office, I tried to work out what I would say when I saw Corinne. But the words were no clearer to me by the time I pulled into the employee lot, and by the time I was cruising up the elevator, my mind began to whir with doubts. What if, despite Aaron being in her life, she just didn't want me in it?

Pushing the last of my doubts away, I stepped into the office, finding the receptionist desk empty, and continued toward my office in the back.

Corinne was here, thank God.

She was alone, standing in the center of my office with her back to me, facing the windows and the view beyond. Her shoulders were tense, and I heard her sniff as if she'd been crying.

"Dove," I said softly, and she turned.

When our eyes met across the office, it was like the air had been sucked from my lungs. Had she always been this beautifully broken?

"Cooper."

I swallowed and wandered closer.

"What are you doing here?" she asked.

I took her hand and led her to the sofa in my office.

We sat down side by side, but with a healthy distance between us. "There are a few things I need to say to you."

She nodded, her eyes filled with a mix of curiosity and regret.

Looking at her with awe, I had to clasp my hands together in my lap to keep from reaching out and touching her. "These last few days without you have been hell. I want you in my life. I need you, Corinne." She opened her mouth to respond, but I shook my head. "The dedication and commitment you've shown to your childhood friend is admirable. It's more than that—it's incredible. It proves what an amazing woman you are. I know you'll never let him go."

She nodded.

"And you don't have to."

Her brows drew together. "I don't understand."

I reached over and took her hand. Having her this near and not touching her, in some small way, was next to impossible.

Corinne took a deep, steadying breath. "It wouldn't be fair to you to continue being your fuck buddy. You deserve it all, Cooper."

I shook my head. "I won't be your fuck buddy. I want to be your everything. There's room for all three of us. I'll help you with Aaron. I would never cast him aside. I know he's important to you."

She licked her lips, thinking it over.

"Quinn looked into it, and the marriage isn't legally binding."

She looked down at her hands. "I know that."

"Little dove. God, I've missed you. Tell me what you're thinking."

She drew another deep inhale. "I've missed you too. But that doesn't change my situation, and there's no way that I could ever ask you to become responsible for both me and another person."

"And there's no way I could ever let you slip away. So I guess we're at an impasse."

At this, she smiled and squeezed my hand. "You really are bossy, you know?"

My gaze met hers, and all the worry I'd felt on the way over here was gone. It had been replaced by a deep sense of peace. This was the right thing, her and me. And

Aaron? Well, it would be no different if she were a single mom with a special-needs child. I'd help her and care for them both—no question. "I love you."

A single tear escaped her eye, and I caught it with my thumb on her cheek. "I love you too," she whispered. "This is so much more than I could have ever expected."

"Corinne? You ready?" Alyssa's voice sounded from outside the office, and when I looked up, she was standing in the doorway. "Oh. Hi, Mr. Kingsley. You're here."

"Give us a minute, would you, Alyssa?"

She nodded and disappeared from the doorway.

I pulled Corinne into my arms and kissed her deeply. "Love you so fucking much," I murmured, my lips teasing hers. She was crying freely now, but I knew they were happy tears.

When Alyssa cleared her throat in the other room, I pulled away. "Later. You're mine."

Corinne nodded, her gaze filled with hot understanding.

I rose to my feet, tugging her up and pulling her

close. "One last thing. Unpack your stuff. You're not quitting."

She laughed, and the sound was pure and sweet. "Yes, sir."

Chapter Twenty-Six

Corinne

My eyes popped open at precisely 5:02 that morning. As I lay there in bed, staring at the ceiling, I could already feel the butterflies swarming in my stomach. The past three weeks had felt like forever, and the day I'd been waiting for was finally here.

Today, Aaron and I were moving in with Cooper.

My whole life was packed up in cardboard boxes, ready to be taken to my new home. Well, maybe not my *whole* life. Cooper was waiting for me with open arms, but I was terrified that the moment I wheeled Aaron through his front door, Cooper would see what kind of life he'd actually signed up for and regret ever inviting us to live with him.

Please, God, or the universe, or whatever power is out there, don't let him regret asking us to move in with him.

The moving truck was set to take our things to Cooper's at ten a.m. sharp. I stayed in bed for another hour, closing my eyes and trying to make myself fall back asleep. But no matter how much I longed for just a little more beauty rest, sleep wouldn't come. Worries kept racing through my mind as I imagined every possible outcome in which moving in with Cooper was a huge mistake.

Even after everything we'd been through, I couldn't silence that small part of me that wondered if Cooper really wanted me in his life—especially now that having me meant having Aaron as well.

When my nervous thoughts became too much, I sprang out of bed and began making one final sweep through the place. As I wandered through the rooms of our apartment, I thought about the life Aaron and I had shared together up until that point.

It had always been just the two of us, from when we were only a couple of nervous kids in the system. Would Aaron be okay with letting another person into our lives? Into my life? I didn't want him to feel replaced or like I didn't care about him in the same way I used to. Moving in with Cooper had so many potential pitfalls.

For as nervous as I was, I was excited to finally get on with it. The anticipation of this day had been killing me.

Once Aaron woke up, I decided to pick up breakfast

sandwiches for us before the moving truck got there. My mind was still racing the entire time, and I was so scattered, I almost forgot to pay for our food. I arrived back home just as the moving truck pulled up, and I hurried inside to let the men in and show them what to do. They were kind and professional, and for just a moment, I felt better about the whole moving process.

They finished loading our boxes into the truck within half an hour, and soon Aaron and I were following the moving truck to our new home.

By the time we pulled up in front of Cooper's building, I felt like my heart was about to pound right through my chest. Cooper was already outside waiting for us, and my stomach dropped at the sight of his wide, welcoming smile. I wheeled Aaron around to the wide front doors while Cooper talked with the moving men and directed them to the service elevator.

With the logistics of the move all worked out, Cooper strode excitedly toward Aaron and me, planting a warm kiss on my cheek and gently patting Aaron's shoulder.

"Ready to see your new home?" Cooper asked, his green eyes bright with anticipation.

I shot him a nervous smile and nodded hesitantly, leaning down to whisper in Aaron's ear, "All right, Aaron, let's take a ride up the elevator."

Cooper led us inside and we ventured up to his floor. Once we reached his penthouse, I was immediately struck by the modifications he had made for the move.

Cooper's home was now perfect for Aaron.

Not only were renovations done so that Aaron could get around more easily, there was even 24/7 care on hand to make sure that all his needs would be met. The doormen were so kind and already knew Aaron and me by name, and the building's security was just strict enough to make the home feel safe. Cooper ushered the morning shift nurse over to us so we could get to know each other, and I could already tell that she was more qualified than I ever imagined possible.

As I went over Aaron's medications and needs with the nurse, Aaron and his therapy dog wandered around the penthouse to get familiar with the space. My stomach churned as the two of them slowly moved through the room. I could only imagine how Aaron might have been feeling.

Was he overwhelmed by all the changes? Did he already hate me for bringing him here, and Cooper for inviting us?

But all my worries faded away when I saw the look on Aaron's face. He was facing the wall of windows that overlooked the busy city streets below, and he looked utterly enamored. Relief flooded through my entire body as I watched a wide grin stretch across his face. I knew then that one of the main men in my life was happy with our new arrangement.

Once I felt that the nurse had a handle on Aaron's needs, I left her to get to know him.

Cooper appeared by my side, placing a steady hand on the small of my back, and I turned to look at him, trying to read if he was already regretting making so much room for another person in our relationship. But all I could see on his face was happiness.

"How are you feeling, little dove?"

I swiped at a stray tear. I wasn't sure when I'd gotten so emotional, but perhaps the buildup of this day had been in my mind for so long, now that it was here and actually going well, relief flooded my system, overwhelming me.

"I feel so blessed. I'm so lucky to have a man like you."

He shook his head, a slow smile uncurling on his lips. "I'm the lucky one, dove. I'm so happy you said yes."

He smiled broadly at me and led me through the living room, pointing out all the ways he'd made his home more wheelchair accessible. Cooper had even modified the master suite, enlarging it so it now had a living area in addition to the bedroom and bathroom. That way, we had our own space and Aaron had his, but we would always be nearby in case he needed us.

It was all perfect—almost too good to be true. How did I find a man so caring and so understanding of my needs?

We spent the rest of the day moving our boxes into their designated rooms, and before I knew it, my stomach was grumbling and I could feel a hunger headache coming on.

"Should we order some pizza?" Cooper asked after unpacking a box full of old photo albums.

"It's like you read my mind," I said, giving him a grateful smile.

We ordered a couple of pizzas, one veggie and one pepperoni. As I organized the last box of the day, out of the corner of my eye, I saw Cooper kneel down next to Aaron's wheelchair. My heart squeezed, and I discreetly moved closer to them to hear what Cooper had to say.

I didn't catch the first thing he said, but as I strained to hear him, I could just make out Cooper's low and steady voice.

"I guess I just wanted to thank you for taking care of her all those years. She's such a special person, and I want you to know that I will protect her, always."

Hearing those words come out of Cooper's mouth and watching him kneeling next to Aaron was almost too much for me to handle, and my vision was soon blurred by the tears welling in my eyes. Cooper was so much more wonderful than I ever could have imagined, and certainly more than I thought I deserved. After everything I put him through, there he was, embracing the man I considered to be my brother, welcoming him into his home and his life with more tenderness and care than I ever could have asked for.

I took a step toward Cooper to thank him, but just as I did, the doorbell rang and he rose to answer it. I smiled and went to Aaron's side instead, crouching down where Cooper had just knelt. I took Aaron's hand in mine and gave it a gentle squeeze. Even though he couldn't squeeze back, I knew that he understood what I was trying to say.

Cooper soon entered the room with two pizza boxes in hand. My mouth instantly started watering from the smell. The three of us sat around the table in our new kitchen, and Aaron's nurse joined us to help him eat his slice. A small pang of guilt shot through me over no longer being the one to help Aaron, but I knew that the small separation would be good for us. I still loved him just as much as I always had, but it was time for me to lead my own life.

While we ate, Cooper and I chatted with Aaron's nurse. I could tell already that she would be a perfect fit. And based on the way Aaron's face lit up whenever she looked at him, I could tell that he liked her too.

Soon after we finished eating, Aaron grew tired, as he usually did after dinner. His nurse wheeled him to his bedroom to get ready to sleep.

I smiled. Maybe this move would work out after all. Aaron had a schedule, and based on the fact that he was already following it, even on our first day here, it was clear that he would have no trouble adjusting. I was happy not only for him, but also for Cooper. I'd been worried that living with Aaron would cramp his style, but I could see now that this new arrangement would work out just fine.

With Aaron gone, it was just Cooper and me at the table. I watched him as he finished his glass of water, a slow smile spreading across my face. He looked up to find me watching him, and he shot me an inquisitive smile.

"What's that look for?" he asked, raising one eyebrow and cocking his head to the side.

"You've been amazing today," I said, my voice low. I placed my elbows on the table and leaned forward a bit, aware of the way the position complemented my breasts.

"Oh, have I?" Cooper smiled and placed his elbows on the table too, mirroring my body language.

We locked eyes, and I remembered what he had said to Aaron earlier. I'd meant to say something to Cooper, to thank him for being so kind and welcoming to the other important man in my life. But as those thoughts ran through my mind, I felt a familiar tingle of desire spread through me, and suddenly I knew exactly how I wanted to reward him.

"Follow me," I said.

Before he could respond, I stood up and grabbed his hand to lead him to the suite he'd designed just for us. When we reached the bedroom, I closed the door behind us. A quick glance at his crotch confirmed my suspicion that his cock was growing harder by the second, a visible bulge appearing behind his zipper. He leaned in to kiss me, but I only allowed his lips to briefly touch mine before I sank to my knees and began to unbutton his jeans.

"You're spoiling me," Cooper said, placing a gentle hand on my head and softly caressing my hair.

"No, I'm rewarding you." I pulled his massive cock out of his pants. No matter how many times I encountered it, the sheer size and girth of his manhood always took my breath away. Without waiting another second, I ran my tongue over the length of his erection, and his cock twitched with desire in response.

"Fuck, little dove," Cooper whispered, moving his

hand to the back of my head and running his fingers through my hair.

I interpreted his touch as encouragement and took his tip between my lips, swirling my tongue around it with varying pressure. Cooper sighed, and his cock quickly grew to its full hardness, just in time for me to take its length in my mouth.

Placing one hand at the base of his cock, I pumped my mouth back and forth over his shaft, working into a rhythm that I knew would only make him want more. I let Cooper's moans tell me when I was doing something right, and relished the feeling of pleasing the man who had done so much for me—both sexually and personally.

Before Cooper, I'd thought that blow jobs were demeaning, but with his giant cock in my mouth, making him groan with pleasure, I'd never felt more empowered—or more convinced that I was exactly where I needed to be.

Chapter Twenty-Seven

Cooper

Wave after wave of pure pleasure washed over me as Corinne worked her pretty little mouth over the length of my cock. If I had known that this was how she'd react to moving in to my home, I would have invited her to move in a long time ago.

The things she was able to do with her mouth were blowing my mind, and my head was spinning with thoughts of the things I wanted to do to repay her.

As her head continued bobbing between my legs, I felt an orgasm building within me. I didn't want her to stop, but if this night was going to go any further, I needed to switch up what was happening. I placed my hand on the back of her head, guiding her away from my cock so I could look her in the eye.

Corinne looked up at me, her eyes wide and eager to please, and I placed two fingers under her chin, motioning for her to rise to her feet. She stood and placed a fervent kiss on my lips, and my cock pulsed when I tasted the subtle tang of salt on her tongue.

This was not the same Corinne I first met in my

office a couple of months ago. She had fully blossomed into the sultry, confident sex goddess I had hoped she would become.

As we continued kissing, I pulled her gray top over her head, and she quickly did the same to me. In one smooth motion, I undid her bra and threw it onto the floor, pulling her into a passionate embrace, reveling in the feel of her skin on mine. Our hands roamed each other's skin, grasping for more of each other, and it wasn't long before I needed more.

I spun her around and threw her on the bed, peeling away her jeans and planting wet kisses up her thighs and onto her abdomen. I kicked off my own pants and carefully pulled her soaking-wet panties down to her ankles. I longed to taste her, and groaned when my mouth met her sweet pussy. She bucked her hips in response, and I reached up to massage her breasts while I worked my tongue over her swollen clit.

Corinne's moans grew louder and more urgent, and I could tell that she was close to orgasm. Just when she was about to come, I stopped and moved up her body, propping up my weight while guiding my needy cock inside her. She gasped and raked her fingernails across my back as I pushed my whole length into her, savoring the way every inch of me was enveloped by her warm and velvety sex.

"Breathe for me, baby," I murmured, knowing whenever I entered her fully like this, it took a moment of adjustment. A moment for her body to accept me.

"Oh my God!" she cried out. "Cooper, it's too much."

I knew what she meant. It felt *too* good. It was hard to handle the flurry of sensations battling for my attention.

"Want me to slow down?" I barely grunted out. She was as tight as a glove, so perfect and lovely. Dropping soft kisses to her mouth, her throat, I thrust slowly— gentle, lazy strokes meant to prepare her for what I needed.

"No. Want it. Want you." She sobbed, her body coaxing me deeper as she tilted her pelvis toward mine.

"Yes." I grunted. "That's it."

We moved together, our bodies remembering this dance, our mouths fused together, our breaths becoming one for several long minutes.

I continued pumping my cock in and out of her until she came in a rush of wet heat, her body tightening wildly around me until she'd successfully milked the orgasm I was desperately trying to hold off.

I came down from my climax as though it was a high, dizzy and euphoric and panting.

"Jesus, Corinne," I murmured, wrapping her in my arms.

We held each other close, cuddling and caressing with the kind of tenderness I'd longed for my entire life. When our pleasure faded into exhaustion, she lifted her head onto my chest, softly stroking the muscles in my chest with her fingertips.

"Thank you," she whispered, her voice breathy, "for being so wonderful with Aaron. I don't think there are enough blow jobs in the world to show you how thankful I truly am."

I chuckled and brushed her hair away from her face so I could see her better. "Don't worry about it," I said, and she raised an inquisitive eyebrow. "I'm not talking about the blow jobs; feel free to keep those coming. I mean about Aaron. I'm a big boy. I wouldn't have asked the both of you to move in if it wasn't what I wanted."

She smiled and raised her mouth to mine, pulling me in for a tender kiss. When we paused to take a breath, I looked deeply into her eyes and knew that this was the moment I'd been waiting for. It was time to ask Corinne the most important question I'd ever ask in my entire life.

"Corinne," I said, placing my hand on her cheek. "There's something I want to ask you."

Her eyes flitted nervously up to mine, and I could have sworn she knew exactly what I was about to say. I felt her heartbeat pick up in her chest, and she cuddled in closer to me as I wrapped my other arm tighter around her.

"You came into my life at a time when I thought I would never be happy again," I said, my heart swelling with love for the gorgeous woman in my arms. "The time I've spent with you has been so much more than I ever hoped it would be. You've shined a light of joy into my life, and for that, I will be forever grateful to you."

Corinne blinked up at me, her eyes slowly filling with tears. I kissed her brow and got up from the bed, opening a drawer in the bedside table and pulling out a small black box. The white duvet was a mess around us, our skin still flushed. But I didn't care. I couldn't wait any longer.

I turned to face her again and Corinne sat up in bed, pulling the sheet over her naked body. A small voice in the back of my head reminded me that I was still naked, that I was about to ask her this question with my cock dangling between my legs, but I didn't care. I had fallen in love with the woman of my dreams, and she miraculously loved me back.

I smiled and knelt before her, and before I even said anything, she clapped her hand over her mouth, tears now freely falling down her cheeks. I opened the little black box and held it up in front of her, smiling at the way the massive diamond glittered, even in the dim moonlight streaming in from the window.

"Little dove, will you marry me?"

Corinne leaped from the bed, throwing her arms around me and planting a flurry of kisses all over my face and neck. I laughed and pulled her into me, our mouths meeting in the deepest, most tender kiss we had shared to date. Tears welled in my own eyes, and I could feel Corinne's happy tears falling onto my chest.

"I'll take that as a yes, then," I said, and we both broke out in laughter, kissing and holding each other as though it was impossible to let go. And it kind of was.

But I pulled back a bit, desperate to see the way my ring looked on her. I slid the ring easily onto her slim finger, silently thanking Mauve for telling me Corinne's ring size.

"Mauve helped you with this, didn't she?" Corinne smiled, running her thumb over my cheek.

I nodded, staring deeply into the eyes of the woman I loved. We continued laughing and kissing until desire overtook us. I picked up my fiancée and laid her gently on our bed, admiring her supple curves and the way her hair fell around her face. We made love in the moonlight, and I knew the life we would build together would be full and happy and beautiful.

I had found her, my one and only.

Knowing she was all mine sent a wave of deep satisfaction throughout my entire body. I felt whole in a way I hadn't before. Content to lie here forever with my fiancée, I drifted off to sleep with my little dove resting on my chest.

Epilogue

Cooper

"Well, Mrs. Kingsley, I have to admit, you throw a damn good party," I said, leaning over to whisper in my wife's ear.

Corinne turned to me and smiled, planting a slow and grateful kiss on my lips. "I still can't believe your brothers paid for all this," she said, looking with wonder around the ornately decorated ballroom.

From the moment I told Gavin and Quinn that Corinne and I were getting married, they demanded that I let them pay for it. They hated the idea of Mauve and Corinne digging into their savings, and wanted to make sure that Corinne got the wedding of her dreams. They could be real dicks sometimes, but every once in a while, my brothers showed me how to be the kind of men we'd all hoped to become after growing up without a father.

And the memory of Quinn and Mauve moving together on the dance floor—that was priceless.

Our ceremony had been short but meaningful. Corinne and I hated the kind of weddings that dragged on and on, so we made sure that ours packed just the right amount of punch in a short amount of time. And I'd be the first to admit that I couldn't stop the tears from falling when I saw Corinne walking down the aisle toward me.

She took my fucking breath away.

I'd known that Corinne was gorgeous from the first moment I met her, but seeing her in that lacy white dress, custom tailored to perfectly hug her jaw-dropping curves . . . it took everything in me not to pause the wedding then and there to find somewhere for us to be alone.

And, honestly, watching Corinne talk to all our family and friends, seeing how she fit in so perfectly with my brothers . . . I had a hard time suppressing that idea at the reception too.

That's why I was so relieved when they began serving dinner, and Corinne and I had a moment to just sit and be together for a while.

"Is it everything you hoped it would be?" Corinne asked, leaning closer to me and placing her hand on my thigh. Even with all the people surrounding us, I couldn't help but notice the subtle twitch in my cock at her touch.

I leaned toward her and smiled, placing my hand over hers and giving it a gentle squeeze. "It's amazing, dove. But you know I would have been happy with a courthouse wedding, as long as it meant that you would be mine—and I would be yours—forever."

Her face softened and she drew my mouth to hers, pulling me into a slow, passionate kiss. When we parted, she raised a mischievous eyebrow. "You have no idea what's in store for you later," she said, her voice low and seductive.

"I think I have some idea," I replied, raising an eyebrow in response.

But before we could discuss our wedding-night plans any further, Gavin and Emma came up to congratulate us, and I could tell from the half-empty glasses in their hands and the slight sheen on both their faces that they'd been enjoying the open bar. They weren't wasted, by any means, but I was glad they were both having fun.

"So, tell me, brother," Gavin said, clapping his hand on my shoulder, a playful grin spreading across his face. "How did you trick this woman into marrying you? It's obvious she's *way* out of your league." He turned and winked at Corinne, and she smiled appreciatively before launching into an excited conversation with Emma about floral designs and the flavor of the cake.

A year and a half ago, it would have been strange to see these two women talking together, so obviously comfortable and friendly with each other. But now that Corinne was my whole world, and my heartbreak over Emma no more than a very distant memory, watching their friendship grow made me incredibly happy. In fact, I felt the same way about Corinne and Emma becoming close as I did about Corinne bonding with my brothers. Emma was family now, and I loved the way she drew Corinne into our family too.

"I don't deserve her," I said, loud enough that Corinne could hear me, "but I'll spend every day of the rest of our lives trying to make it so I do."

Corinne turned to smile at me before placing another kiss on my lips. Gavin put his arm around Emma and kissed her cheek as well. He looked from Emma to Corinne before turning to me, his eyes serious.

"Mom would be proud," Gavin said, his voice dropping.

I nodded, and our wives exchanged sad smiles. Corinne took my hand in hers.

"To Mom," I said, raising my glass in the air. "And to

your parents, Corinne. I know they would be proud of the woman you've become."

Corinne, Gavin, and Emma all raised their glasses with me, and we appreciated the bittersweet moment together. Corinne used her napkin to dab at the corner of her eyes, and I squeezed her hand in mine to comfort her. We had both lost so much in our pasts, which made it all the sweeter that we'd found each other.

Shortly after our toast, Gavin and Emma returned to their seats at the wedding-party table, between Quinn and Aaron. It warmed my heart to see Emma interact so kindly with Aaron, and I could tell from Corinne's tender gaze that she appreciated the way Aaron had been welcomed into the family as well.

While it would have been nice to be sitting in the midst of our closest family and friends, I was glad Corinne and I decided to sit at a separate table by ourselves for the reception. The day was already so jam-packed with greetings, well wishes, and conversations with people we hadn't seen in years, it was nice to have a space for just the two of us.

As we finished eating our dinner, old friends and family members continued dropping by our table, offering their congratulations and giving us advice about how to make it last. Soon enough, we were cutting the cake and sharing our first dance out on the dance floor. The reception flew by in a blur of laughter and kisses. I'd always been a bit of a romantic at heart, and my wedding day surpassed even my wildest dreams.

As the night wound down and our guests began to trickle out of the ballroom, I grew more and more excited for everyone to leave. Corinne thought that I'd booked us the honeymoon suite at the nicest hotel in Boston. I told her I had something special planned, and she knew that I loved to spoil her. What she didn't know, however?

I had a different destination in mind. One we needed to board a plane later to get to.

In the year and a half that we'd known each other, Corinne still hadn't traveled outside the country. While I let her make almost all the decisions about our wedding, I reserved the honeymoon planning for myself. Our relationship had started with me opening Corinne up to new experiences and new pleasure. I couldn't wait to expand her horizons even further.

My favorite part? She had no idea what was coming.

After hugging our families good-bye, Corinne and I climbed into the back of a limo and settled back into our seats. She nestled into my side, my perfect little dove, and I placed a firm and loving kiss on her head.

She peered up at me, her eyes full of love. "Today was magical. I feel so blessed. I love you, Coop."

"I love you more, little dove." This time, I drew her mouth up to meet mine. We shared a deep kiss, and as her tongue slid against mine, I let out a soft groan.

"You are exquisite," I said, pulling back. "But we need to stop or I'm not going to be fit to be seen in public."

Her gaze lowered to my lap and she gave me a knowing grin. "That thing is hard to hide."

"That thing?" I smirked, teasing her. As much as she'd opened up sexually, she still rarely called body parts by their proper word. "It's a cock, baby. And it's all for you."

She patted my thigh. "Later, big boy. He'll live until then, won't he?"

"Barely," I murmured. I'd been waiting all day to have her.

"So, when will you tell me which hotel we're going to?" she asked, tracing the outline of my palm with her fingers.

I smiled. "We're not going to a hotel tonight, dove."

Corinne looked at me, her eyes wide, a smile tugging at the corners of her mouth. "Where are we going then? And what about our bags? I thought you dropped them off this morning."

"I did drop our bags off," I murmured, raising my eyebrows in amusement. "Just not where you were expecting."

"Cooper Kingsley, you are killing me." Corinne huffed, pulling her hand away from mine. "You know I hate surprises."

I chuckled. "Well, Mrs. Kingsley, you promised you'd let me surprise you. And trust me, you're going to like this one."

Just as I finished speaking, we pulled into the parking lot of the hangar, and I climbed out of the limo, helping Corinne out behind me. The moment she stepped out of the car, Corinne gasped, taking in the sight of the luxury private jet for the first time.

"Cooper," she whispered, her eyes welling with tears. "This must have cost you a fortune! I know that Forbidden Desires does well, but this . . . this is a whole other level of expensive," she said, her eyes glazing over a bit at the thought of the money.

"One of our clients offered his plane," I said, shrugging my shoulders. "Our bags are already on board. I thought we could use a real getaway. We'll spend the week on the beach in the Bahamas."

Corinne didn't say anything, just continued looking up at me with wide, searching eyes.

"If that's okay with you, Mrs. Kingsley." My lips twitched into a smile.

Corinne gasped and quickly threw her arms around me, pulling me in for a passionate kiss. She was laughing, and her eyes were filled with tears. "No one's ever done anything like this for me before."

In that moment, with her looking so soft and vulnerable, I couldn't help myself. Cupping her cheek, I leaned in and took her bottom lip between my teeth, nipping her gently.

Her breath caught as her tongue swept out and

touched mine without hesitation.

I'd kissed her before so many times, but it had never been like this. The guarded carefulness of her touch had faded, replaced with a full-on openness that hadn't been there before.

I breathed her in, knowing that she was really and truly mine. Her tongue stroked mine again and I pulled her deeper still, tugging her closer until our chests were pressed together . . . until I could feel her heartbeat against my own.

This.

This was what true love and acceptance felt like.

I'd waited so long to find it, to feel it, and I still never could have imagined how whole and peaceful it made me feel.

"I love you, little dove," I whispered.

With tears in her eyes, Corinne blinked at me solemnly. "I don't know what I did to deserve you, but I promise to make you the happiest man in the world, sweet husband."

I gathered her close. "You already have."

Up Next in This Series

Tempting Little Tease

She's the tutor I hired to teach me Italian.

She's way too young for me, but she's also gorgeous, bright, and filled with a curiosity about life that I find incredibly refreshing.

It's fucking adorable.

I'm old enough to know better, but this pretty young thing tempts me beyond belief. And for the first time in my life, I can see myself falling.

• • •

Is this what it's like to be pursued by an older man? The complete confidence, the lack of expectations, the sincerity?

My God, it's exhilarating.

Quinn Kingsley is totally unexpected. I'm moving to Italy in three weeks to teach English, and while I never expected something so real to develop between us so quickly, our chemistry is undeniable.

There's something so sexy about this back-and-forth he and I share. Flirting with this man is like playing with fire, and I'm bound to get burned.

Io sono attratto da te. I'm attracted to you, he tells me.

But is our attraction enough to get us through the complications of a massive age gap and an international love affair? Only one way to find out . . .

Also in This Series

Dirty Little Secret

Dirty Little Promise

Torrid Little Affair

Tempting Little Tease

Acknowledgments

A massive thank-you to the following people for helping this story come to life:

First, to my amazing publicist and right hand in all the things, Danielle Sanchez. When I mentioned this story idea I had for three brothers who owned an escort agency, and you said, "Ohhh, you should write that next," your enthusiasm was the reason I did.

A huge tackle-hug and a glass of fizzy champagne to all the readers who purchased a copy. You are the reason I get to continue bringing my stories to life. I truly hope you loved this one as much as I did, and I can't wait to bring you more.

Up next is Quinn's book, and I'm loving the story already.

Printed in Great Britain
by Amazon

Other Books by Kendall Ryan

Unravel Me

Make Me Yours

When I Break Series

Filthy Beautiful Lies Series

The Gentleman Mentor

Sinfully Mine

Bait & Switch

Slow & Steady

The Room Mate

The Play Mate

The House Mate

The Bed Mate

The Soul Mate

Hard to Love

The Fix Up

For a complete list of Kendall's books, visit:

http://www.kendallryanbooks.com/all-books/

About the Author

A *New York Times*, *Wall Street Journal*, and *USA TODAY* bestselling author of more than two dozen titles, Kendall Ryan has sold over two million books, and her books have been translated into several languages in countries around the world. Her books have also appeared on the *New York Times* and *USA TODAY* bestseller list more than three dozen times. Ryan has been featured in publications such as *USA TODAY*, *Newsweek*, and *In Touch Magazine*. She lives in Texas with her husband and two sons.

Website: www.kendallryanbooks.com